FRAT HOUSE CONFESSIONS: RIDGE

FRAT HOUSE CONFESSIONS, BOOK 1

BETHANY LOPEZ

Frat House Confessions: Ridge
Copyright 2019 Bethany Lopez
Published June 2019
ISBN - 9781072926436
Cover Design by Makeready Designs
Editing by Red Road Editing / Kristina Circelli
Formatting by Bethany Lopez

All rights reserved. No part of this book may be reproduced, scanned, or distributed in any printed or electronic form without permission. Please don't participate in or encourage piracy of copyrighted materials in violation of the author's rights. Purchase only authorized editions.

This is a work of fiction. Names, characters, places, and incidents either are the product of the author's imagination or are used fictitiously, and any resemblance to actual persons, living or dead, businesses, companies, events, or locales is entirely coincidental.

Want to learn more about my books? Sign up for my newsletter and Join my FB Group/Street Team!
https://landing.mailerlite.com/webforms/landing/r7w3w5
https://www.facebook.com/groups/1443318612574585/

 Created with Vellum

*To anyone who yearns to be accepted and love for who they are...
you deserve it. Don't settle for anything less.*

PROLOGUE

"Forgive me, Papi, for I have sinned," I said dryly, sneering at the bottle in my hand, whose contents were dwindling.

"Tell me," Papi asked.

Papi was our treasurer. He'd originally planned on becoming a priest, and now was our go-to guy for advice, complaints, and absolution for our sins. We all knew that he'd given up the priesthood, but we still used his room as the frat house confessional.

"I've been having those urges again," I muttered.

"About your father?" he pressed, leaning forward in his chair with his elbows resting on his knees.

He was currently dressed in a toga.

Not to be a total fucking cliché, but it was rush week and as the hottest frat on campus it was our duty to host the first toga party of the season.

"Yeah," I replied, taking a chug of rum before adding, "The one where I beat him bloody."

"Has something happened to bring these thoughts back? You were doing good over the summer, and hadn't thought about him or the way he'd treated you as a child for a while. I thought our talks were helping."

"They are, it's just ... Brody called to give me and Wes a head's up ... My mom's filing for divorce. Guess the bastard's been cheating on her again. And, that's not all, Brody heard them fighting and found out the asshole was married before."

"No shit?" Papi asked, his face showing his surprise.

I couldn't blame him. I thought I knew every skeleton in my father's closet.

"Yeah, turns out we have three older sisters."

Brody and Wes were my younger brothers. Wes was here at college with me, while Brody was living out the last year of his sentence in that mausoleum our parents called a home.

"Fuck, that's crazy," Papi said, taking a pull of his beer.

I ran my hand over my face, my vision blurring as I recalled my conversation with Brody.

"Now, my mom's feeling all clingy and emotional and said Wes and I have to come home for Thanksgiving. She's talking about inviting her best friend and her daughter, who she's been trying to hook me up with for years. She's always had this grand plan of marrying me off and partnering up with another rich family who have good social connections. I don't know how I'm going to get out of it."

Papi leaned back and teepee'd his hands, bringing them to his lips as he looked at me thoughtfully.

I took another drink as I waited, sure that Papi would bring the magic like he always did.

A few seconds later, he snapped his fingers and stood up excitedly.

"I've got it."

"Tell me," I encouraged, getting to my feet as well, albeit somewhat unsteadily.

"Two birds ... one stone."

I waited, the sounds of the music from below pulsing beneath my feet.

"This year, Crush is planning on making the pledges participate in a new test. Each pledge is going to have to find a girl who needs help. You know, somewhat dumpy, shy, or in that awkward, *I just moved away from home and don't know who I am phase*. Once they get their pick approved, it will be their job to make her over and turn her into the kind of chick we'd want hanging around the house, rather than the type to hang with the losers in Denny's all night."

"What, like a dogfight? That's fucked up," I said with a scowl.

Crush was a fucking asshole, but everyone knew that.

"Kind of, but not quite that shitty. We aren't giving out prizes for finding the ugliest chick and making her think she's hot, we're rewarding pledges who find a girl with *potential* and help her realize that potential."

"How do I play into it?"

"Well, as the brother every pledge wants to emulate, and our Sergeant at Arms, you could sort of *lead the cause*. Get Crush off your ass by playing along with his stupid game. Find a girl to makeover, let Crush have his jollies, and take the girl to Thanksgiving. Tell your mom you guys are in love and she doesn't need to fix you up."

I looked at him like he was crazy, *cause he fucking is*, then shook my head.

When the room started spinning, I stopped.

"I can't take some frumpy girl home for Thanksgiving. My mom will never fall for that shit. She is *the* Susan Temple after all, and anything other than a Stepford chick will not be welcome."

"Ridge, *dude*, you're not listening," Papi said, then looked at me closely and added, "Or, maybe you're just drunk ... You will make this girl into whoever you want her to be. Make her over into the young woman of Susan Temple's wet dreams."

"That's fucking gross," I said with a scowl.

"Just think about it," Papi said. "That's your penance, if you choose to accept it. Find a college beauty who's hiding her light under a bushel and give her a makeover that'll have every guy in this house jizzing over her."

He walked over to the door and opened it, turning back to me.

"Now, we have a kickass party going on downstairs, and I just know there are some fine ladies down there wondering where their Papi went, so I'm going down. You coming?"

"Nah," I said as I followed him into the hall. "I'm not really feelin' it. I think I'm gonna go listen to some music and sort my shit out. If anyone asks where I am, just say I'm balls deep in a blonde."

"You got it, brother," Papi said, bounding down the stairs toward the chaos.

I turned left down the hall toward my room, swaying slightly as I lifted the bottle once more to my lips, and wondered if I was willing to lie to some unsuspecting chick in order to get my mom off my back.

Probably.

ONE

KARRIE

"*What are we doing in here?*"
"*I have a surprise for you...*"

I watched everything playing out on the tiny screen of my phone, like a car accident that I knew was coming, but couldn't tear my eyes away.

The girl with her eyes dancing, all dressed up in her LBD and heels, excited about what she had in store for her boyfriend, was me ... silly, naïve, Karrie, who was about to have her heart shattered.

The handsome boy, who we all now knew was a total asshole, was my then boyfriend, Drake. He was about to pull my heart from my chest and hand it back to me.

It had been four months, and I'd had the entire summer to get over it, but for some reason, whenever I got low, I pulled up the video and reminded myself why men could not be trusted.

I blinked back tears and focused on the oblivious girl.

I cringed as I caught my wink toward where I'd set my phone up to record, eager to get Drake's reaction when I gave him his present.

"Karrie, since we're alone, there's been something I've been meaning to tell you," Drake began, and I held my breath as I waited for him to drop the bomb on my unsuspecting self.

"What's that?" I asked innocently.

I'd literally had no idea that there was anything wrong in our relationship. We'd dated exclusively all of sophomore year after he'd swept me off my feet at the field party after the last softball game of the season.

"I think we should see other people," Drake said, and a tear slipped down my cheek as I watched myself blink at him, not sure I'd heard him correctly.

"What? Why would we do that?" my former self asked.

"Because we've only got two years left of school, and it's crazy for us to be tied down, don't you think? I mean, don't you want to see what else is out there?"

"No, of course not ... and neither do you ... *Drake*, we love each other. Please, don't do this," I pleaded and I wanted to reach in the phone and clap my hand over my mouth. Urge myself to shut up and not sound so desperate.

"I'm sorry, Karrie, but I can't do this anymore," Drake had said, then he walked past me and out the door without looking back.

Unfortunately, I'd forgotten all about the video I'd been recording, so there was ten more minutes of footage where I cried my eyes out. I mean, full-on snot bubbles and all.

I never watched that part. I didn't need to. I knew it was there, and that was humiliating enough.

"Please tell me you're not watching that video again."

I looked up to see my roommate, Ermina, glaring at me from the kitchen.

I quickly exited out of my videos and dropped the phone on the couch.

"Karrie, why do you do that to yourself? Drake is a total douche, don't let his actions keep controlling your emotions."

Ermina was studying psychology and I was her favorite test subject.

"I'm not. I just needed a reminder of why men are pigs," I replied.

Ermina sighed.

"All men are not like Drake and you need to stop lumping them all together. You're going to find someone to treat you the way you deserve to be treated."

"Right now, I'd just settle for making Drake see what a mistake he made, then shove his face in it."

"You're better than that," Ermina chastised.

"You know, I don't think I am," I countered, but she just laughed.

I noticed she was dressed up to go out and asked, "Where are you off to?"

"Well, as you know, it's rush week, so I planned on heading out to a party so I could study the animals in their natural habitat ... maybe find a topic for my research paper. Wanna join me?"

She asked it reluctantly, and I knew it was because I'd said no every time she'd asked me to do anything over the last four months.

It's time for that to change, I decided and stood up.

"You know what, I will go with you," I replied, and her jaw dropped.

"Really?" Ermina asked, her voice conveying her excitement.

"Yeah, let me throw on some shorts and I'll be ready."

She looked down at my favorite T-shirt and ratty sweat pants, then up at my hair, which was pulled up in a bun, and said, "I can wait while you put some clothes on, maybe do your hair and makeup."

"Nah, I'm good," I replied, pushing my glasses up my nose, not caring what I looked like.

I just needed to get out of this apartment ... maybe have a drink, *or ten*.

I hadn't gone to a party as a single woman since Drake and I'd broken up and hadn't been to a party without him in over a year.

"Okay, as long as you get out of the house, I'll take you however I can get you," Ermina said, and I blew her a kiss.

"I'll be ready in five."

Three minutes later we were out the door and headed to Greek Row, ready to mingle with the elitists and the poor underclassmen who desperately wanted to join them. I didn't care about fraternities or sororities, how they acted or what went on behind closed doors, all I cared about was free booze and wiping Drake from my memory.

TWO
KARRIE

"Thank you," I said to the pledge who handed me a beer, then turned around, scanned the room, and exclaimed, "You've got to be kidding me!"

"What?" Ermina asked, turning to follow my gaze.

"Fucking Drake," I whispered, closing my eyes to try and shut out the sight of the well-chiseled jaw and curly brown hair of my ex.

"Shit, seriously?" Ermina asked. "I thought he never came to frat parties."

"He never used to stand in the middle of the room with his tongue down some half-dressed, big-titted chick either, but he's doing that right now."

"*Shit*," Ermina said, a little louder this time, and began ushering me into a different room.

Once we were in the crowded dining room, where a rousing game of beer pong was happening, Ermina looked at me and said, "Let me go get a closer look, you stay in here. *Don't move.*"

I leaned against the wall, then thought better of it and stood straight. *Who knows what these Delta guys do on the walls.*

After a few seconds, I could no longer resist the urge and

peered around the corner back into the other room, to see what Ermina and Drake were doing. He was no longer lip-locked, but instead was scowling at my roommate, who was standing before him with her hands on her hips. She appeared to be reading him the riot act.

I love Ermina.

I grinned and started to slide back into my spot, only to find it was currently occupied.

"Oh, sorry," I said when I stepped on someone's foot.

I looked first at the foot, which was large and encased in basketball shoes, then my gaze traveled up the thick jean-clad thighs, over a form-fitting T-shirt, which did nothing to hide the well-formed chest underneath, before landing on a very handsome face.

"No problem," the sexy stranger said with a lopsided grin, which only made him more handsome. "Did I take your spot?"

I shrugged and took a sip of my beer as I looked around the room. "There's plenty of wall space."

"Hmmm, but, why are you hanging out by the wall?" he asked, his voice deep and kinda gravely.

"Where should I be hanging out?" I asked, wondering what was taking Ermina so long.

"I'm sure any guy here would be pleased as fuck if you spent some time with them," the sexy stranger said, and I knew immediately he was full of shit.

I rolled my eyes and said, "Give me a break."

"What?" he asked innocently.

I waved a hand over myself and shot him a glare.

I knew I didn't look my best. Hell, I didn't look *Ermina's* worst.

"What's your game?" I asked him.

"What makes you think I'm playin'?"

I took in his short dark hair, bright blue eyes, almost too-perfect face, and rolled my eyes again.

Unable to stand it any longer, I ignored him and peeked into the other room again.

"Who are we looking at?"

I glanced over to see ole blue eyes peering over my shoulder.

"That asshole?" he scoffed. "From the baseball team? You can do better than him."

I looked up at the side of his face. "You know Drake?"

"Yeah, he comes around here a lot. Thinks he's big man on campus and that by hanging with us, he's one of us ... but it doesn't work that way. He's a total knob."

"He comes here a lot?" I repeated, looking back at Drake and wondering if I ever really knew him. "You mean, this year?"

"This year. Last year. Ever since he started school here. He's always here hanging on some different girl. Like I said, you could do better."

I gasped and looked back at him, shocked.

"*Last* year he was here? With a different girl every time?" I asked, my voice loud enough to make people look over at us.

He nodded.

"*Mother fucker*," I hissed, then tossed back my beer, threw the red solo cup on the ground, and stormed over to where Ermina was still giving Drake the business.

"*You cheating asshole!*" I shouted when I was close enough.

"Karrie, what the fuck?" Drake asked, looking around, seeming embarrassed I was making a scene. "We aren't dating anymore, I can see who I want."

"Not now, douche nozzle, *before*, when we *were* together," I clarified, stopping before him and putting my hands on my hips. "My new friend over there said you were always coming in here with strange women, even when you were supposed to be committed to me."

Drake looked over my head and scowled.

"You believe fucking *Ridge*? Dude's the biggest player around."

"I don't care if he gets more action than Dwayne Johnson, I'm more worried about what *you* were doing."

Drake clasped his hand around my bicep and started dragging me down the hall.

I squirmed and tried to get loose, but his grip was too strong.

"Get your hands off her!" Ermina yelled, her heels clapping down the hall as she ran after us.

Before I could jerk my arm away, my blue-eyed stranger was standing before us, glaring down at Drake.

Call me petty, but I liked the fact that he towered over Drake.

"Unhand her, man, that's not how we treat women at Delta."

Surprisingly, Drake let me go, before turning on his heel to go back the way he came.

"Keep your crazy away from me, Karrie, yeah? We're over. Let it go," he said over his shoulder and he was gone.

"You okay?"

I rubbed my bicep absently and finally asked, "Who are you?"

"My name is Ridge, and I have a proposition for you."

THREE
RIDGE

"Uh, looks like you got it handled," Karrie's hot friend said, then clicked off toward the party.

I looked down at the skeptical girl in front of me and suppressed a grin.

She may have been wearing glasses, unfortunate clothes, and not an ounce of makeup, but even with her hair piled on her head, I could tell she could be seriously hot with a little effort.

This would be almost too easy ... if I could get her to play along.

"What sort of *proposition*?" Karrie asked warily.

"Come upstairs with me, so we can get some privacy, and I'll tell you all about it."

"Upstairs? Yeah, right. Why would I go upstairs alone with you? What do you think I am ... stupid or easy?" she asked, and I bit back an impatient retort.

"Neither. It'll be quiet, and we won't have so many eyes on us. What I want to ask needs to be done in private," I said.

When she looked like she wanted to argue some more, I looked her pointedly up and down and added, "Don't worry, I just want to talk. You're not my type."

Karrie scoffed, looking momentarily offended.

I worried I'd been too honest, but then she shrugged and said, "After you. But, I'm texting my friend to let her know where I am, so she knows who to come after if anything happens."

"Works for me."

I grabbed a couple beers on the way up and led her to my room.

My mom had raised me to always make my bed and put things in their place, so I wasn't worried about freaking her out with my piggish ways, like some of my brothers.

"Hey, Ridge!"

I looked down over the railing into the room below, to see Crush looking at Karrie's back and giving me a thumb's up sign.

Then he fisted his hands and gyrated them like he was fucking the air from behind.

What an ass.

I ignored him and kept on walking.

Once we were to my door, I opened it and stepped aside to let Karrie walk in first.

"Wow, this is nice," she commented, the surprise evident in her voice. "It doesn't even stink. Drake's room always smelled like sweaty socks. I always came armed with room spray."

"Take a seat," I said, ignoring her comment as I shut the door behind us.

Karrie looked at the bed, then at my desk chair, before choosing comfort and opting for the bed.

"Okay, I'm here. What's the proposition?" she asked, accepting the beer I offered.

"First, let me ask you to hear me out, *all of it*, before you bust in all pissed and say no."

"That sounds ominous," Karrie said, and I chuckled. "But, yeah, okay ... go ahead."

I paced the room for a minute, then grabbed my desk chair and placed it in front of her. I sat down, keeping my eyes on hers, and prayed she was as cool as I suspected she was, and wasn't about to kick me in the nuts or something.

"*Here it goes* ... Crush, our VP and resident dick, has the pledges picking girls to give makeovers to. The pledge that makes the biggest transformation, wins, although, I have no fucking idea what the prize is ... probably to wash Crush's jock strap or something. Anyway, Crush and I don't see eye to eye, and he's been making noise about trying to get me fired as Sergeant at Arms so he can find someone to take my place who will do whatever he says. It was suggested to me, that if I play along and lead this stupid game, it'll keep him off my back, at least this year. The position looks good on my resume, or I wouldn't care, but I'm not gonna let that douche mess things up for me."

Karrie looked more and more pissed as I talked, so when I paused, I held up my hand and said, "I'm not done yet."

She stuck out her tongue, then bit down on it to let me know she was keeping her promise.

"I need to take someone home with me for Thanksgiving, to keep my mom off my back about settling down, even though I'm not even done with school yet. She's a little crazy and is adamant that I get married right after graduation. Since I'm not prepared to pick out my wife just yet ... that's where you come in."

I stopped talking, and when Karrie stayed silent, I said, "Okay, you can stop biting your tongue now."

"What's in it for me?" she asked, and I felt relieved that she didn't automatically shut me down.

I didn't know her well, but the fact that she was hiding her light under a bushel, and I could offer her something in return, made my job much easier. I'd rather not lie to some unsuspecting chick about Crush's stupid game, and I didn't want to pick one of the frat house groupies who may think I'd come to actually like them.

Karrie was obviously bitter, and still hung up on that douche Drake, which made her perfect for my plan.

"Drake and I hate each other. Like, *I fucking can't stand him*. From what I can tell, you and he were a couple and not only did you not know he was stepping out on you the whole time, but things didn't end well. If he thinks you're with me, it'll drive him crazy."

"Hmmm, I'm listening," Karrie said, tossing back more beer.

"You'll get to hang out here, which means free food and all the booze you can drink. Plus, I'll pay for the makeover. That includes, clothes, makeup, hair ... You'll be set for the year."

I looked her over again. She obviously needed some help putting herself together, and I had money to spare.

"And, we'll pretend to date," she clarified.

"Yup."

"What about this stupid makeover thing for your hazing, what do I have to do for that?" she asked.

"It's not a hazing, just a mess around," I said, not wanting that shit to get around. Hazing was illegal on campus and they wouldn't hesitate to shut us down. "You'd come to the initial party next week, where all the pledges and brothers who are playing bring their girls and we take their before pictures. Then, in two months, we'll have the big reveal, where we'll show off the transformation and take the after pictures. There'll be some sort of ceremony where Crush gets up in front of everyone so he can hear himself talk, and then he gives out prizes to the girls and pledges."

"Then, Thanksgiving."

"Yup, Chicago for Thanksgiving. And, after that, it's over. We'll stage a breakup and you can go back to your life."

Karrie stood up and I followed suit.

"Can I think about it?" she asked.

"Of course. Why don't I give you my number and you can call me with your answer? I just need to know before the party on Friday."

I watched as she input my number into her phone, then walked her to the door.

"Thanks for hearing me out," I said, but Karrie just nodded and gave me a small smile, before walking out and disappearing down the hall.

I shut the door and leaned against in, sending up a small prayer that she'd say yes.

She's the one, I know it.

FOUR
KARRIE

"How's it going, sweetheart? You doing well in your classes?"

"Mom," I chided. "School barely started."

"I know, honey, but your scholarship..."

"I've been doing this for three years now, I know what I need to do to keep my scholarship."

"Sorry, force of habit."

"Yeah, it's okay, I'm used to it," I joked. "How's Carter doing?"

My brother, Carter, was fifteen and a teenage nightmare. He and I had always been close, but my parents were having a hard time with him.

My mom sighed.

"The same. Basically stays in his room all day and grunts at us when we try and talk to him."

"Is that Karrie?" I heard my dad ask in the background.

"Yes, Judd, I'm not done..."

"I just want to say hi before I head out, Sam."

I smiled at their bickering.

"Hey, baby girl, how's practice going?"

I rolled my eyes and laughed.

While my mom was always worried about my schoolwork, my dad only cared about softball.

"So far so good. It's been great seeing everyone again, and meeting the new team members."

"Coach still got you at short stop?" he asked, and the fact that we'd had this conversation a million times over the years brought me comfort.

"Yup, that's what she said last practice."

"That's good. Make sure you're warming up good every time, even if you're just running drills."

My dad had played baseball in college and had even gone pro for a while, but had given it all up for me and my mom. He'd gone on to coach at the high school he was a teacher at, and coached me growing up.

There'd never been any question about it, I was always going to be a softball player.

"I know, Dad, I will... promise."

"Okay, Kare-bear, love you, here's your mom back."

"I love you too, Dad."

"I'm back," my mom said eagerly, and I felt bad when I informed her, "Mom, I've got to go. My first class is in fifteen."

"Oh, okay, honey, you have a good day, and we'll talk again soon."

"Thanks, Mom, love you."

"I love you, too."

I hung up and picked up my bag as I headed for the door.

"I wish I had parents like yours," Ermina said groggily.

My eyes flew to where she stood in the kitchen, coffee cup in hand.

"Jeez, I didn't know you were standing there!" I exclaimed, my hand going to my heart.

"Mmmm, I was eavesdropping while you talked to your hot dad."

"Gross."

I curled my lip up at her as I put my hand on the door handle.

"I gotta go," I told her, and added, "And, your parents are great."

She huffed. "My parents are more worried about whether or not I'm tarnishing their good name than how I'm doing in my classes. They're nothing like your parents."

I didn't have time to argue or talk up her parents, so I simply said, "Make sure you make it to class on time. I'll see you tonight."

"'Kay."

I was hurrying to the English building when a large mass stepped into my path.

I looked up, pulled the earbuds out of my ears, and blinked at the sexy crooked grin from the other night.

"Hey," I said, cringing when it came out more breathless than I'd intended.

"Hey yourself," Ridge replied with a grin, giving me a onceover.

I was suddenly very aware of the fact that I was wearing the same T-shirt from the party, my hair was pulled back in a makeshift bun, and my face was once again makeup free.

Feeling self-conscious, which only made me defensive, I glared up at him.

"Get a good look?" I asked. "I bet you're happy I look like this ... It falls right into your makeover plan."

Ridge cocked a dark eyebrow.

"Does that mean you're going to go along with it?"

I'd told him I'd think about it and get back to him before the party, but I was still on the fence.

"Not sure yet," I said, before darting around him.

Within seconds he'd fallen into step beside me. "What do you have going on today?" he asked.

"Why?"

"Cause a boyfriend should know his girl's schedule," Ridge said with a cocky grin.

"Ugh," was my reply.

"Come on, it won't hurt you to tell me..."

No longer hearing him, I stopped in my tracks when I saw Drake and the girl from the party. They were walking up the steps to the English building. He was smiling down at her, and she up at him.

When he opened the door for her and followed her inside, the breath came back into my lungs and I became aware of Ridge talking.

"Karrie."

I blinked and looked up at him.

A thousand pictures flashed through my mind.

Drake and I at the fields after my games, Drake telling me he loved me as he hovered over me in bed, and Drake smiling at the girl who'd replaced me.

"Okay," I told Ridge, my mind made up for me. "You have a deal. I'll be your makeover project and go home with you for Thanksgiving, *if* you help me make Drake wish he'd never even heard my name."

FIVE
RIDGE

"Ridge."

I was heading upstairs to my room when I heard my brother call my name.

I looked down to see Wes, my younger brother, and soon to be *frat* brother, leaving a group of pledges and heading my way.

"Hey, Wes, what's up?" I asked as I turned and headed back down the stairs.

Wes was a freshman this year, and first up on his agenda was to become a Delta. I'd encouraged it because having a group of brothers behind him would not only keep him motivated, but it was a good way for Wes to meet people and get involved.

He was planning on going out for the swim team, since he'd been on the team in high school, but being a swimmer wasn't going to get him pussy, especially as a freshman. Being a Delta, however, now that would have all the ladies fighting to get a taste.

"Crush said you'd be at the party tonight, that you're entering a girl into the contest."

"Nah, we're not entering, I'm just playing along to ... show solidarity, if you will. It'll still be a pledge event. Why, worried about a little competition?" I joked, even though I knew that's not what he meant.

Wes was the middle child, the *good* one. He was Mom's favorite and the peacekeeper in the family. I was hoping getting him out of her clutches would give him the chance to loosen up for once.

"I don't know how I feel about the whole thing ... seems kinda dickish," Wes said quietly, looking around to make sure no one heard him.

Namely Crush.

"It is, but we won't let it get out of hand. Crush may be an idiot, but he's not malicious ... Antoine would never have signed off on something that could be seen as hazing or bullying," I assured him.

Antoine was our president, and nothing happened in Delta without his approval.

"Do you have a girl picked out already?"

Wes sucked in air and blew out his cheeks like a blowfish. It's a nervous thing he'd done since we were kids.

Having him here, at Delta with me, was actually extremely satisfying to me, and I hadn't thought it would be. Given the fact that I'd grown up as Dad's punching bag and he'd always been shielded behind Mom's skirts, my brother and I didn't have the best relationship.

But, we were both growing up, out of the asylum of our childhood, and finally getting to know each other as people.

Logically, I knew it wasn't his fault he was Mom's favorite. And, honestly, I'd rather be the one taking the hits and keep my brothers safe, but after years of bruises, welts, and broken bones, logic didn't always factor.

I'd been jealous of my brothers, and so eager to get away the ink had barely dried on my diploma before I was gone.

After a few months, I'd started to worry that without me

there, my father's anger would turn to Wes or Brody; luckily, that hadn't happened. Mom had finally put her foot down and stood up to our dad, and he'd apparently lost interest and started sleeping around ... finding his jollies elsewhere.

We were all better off without him in our lives.

"Yeah, there's this girl in my Lit class, she's pretty cool. I told her about this competition and although she's not into Greek Row, she *does* need help with something, so we're gonna trade."

"What does she need help with?" I asked, hoping some chick wasn't taking advantage of him already. "Is she a good fit for the comp? Cause Crush takes this shit very seriously."

"Huh? Oh, yeah, she's a good fit. She's not interested in a makeover, but said she'll play along if I help her pick up chicks?" Wes replied, not taking his eyes off the ground.

I chuckled.

"*Wait*, she wants *you* to help her get women?" I asked incredulously. "And, how are you going to do that? With your vast knowledge of eighties movies?"

Unless things had changed drastically in the two years since I'd left home, I knew Wes was the last person anyone should ask for dating advice.

My brother had zero game.

"I know how to talk to girls," Wes protested.

"Dude, you dated one girl in high school, Cynthia, and you knew her your whole life. All you guys did was eat lunch together at school one day and boom, you were dating. Have you ever even asked someone out on a date."

Wes thinned his lips and I knew I was right.

"You better be careful," I warned him, placing my hand on his shoulder. "College chicks are different than high school. They may be just a few months older, but something happens when they get out on their own. If you don't deliver what she's asking, there's bound to be some blowback. Especially if she comes through for you."

"It'll be fine," he said, shrugging my hand off. "She's a nice person, you'll see."

I lifted a shoulder.

What could I do? I'd warned him, now he was on his own.

"All right, well, I'm gonna go get ready, I'll see you at the party," I said, but before I could turn and head back up, he stopped me.

"Hey, have you heard from Brody?"

"Nah, not in a couple weeks. Why?" I asked.

"Mom said he's acting weird ... staying out all night, hanging out with guys she doesn't know. She's worried."

"I'm sure he's fine," I scoffed. "He's a senior for God's sake, what does she expect, him to be home sitting down with her for dinner at the formal table, serving her cocktails?"

"Ridge," Wes warned, his tone impatient. "She's not as bad as you make her out to be."

"Actually, she's worse," I replied, and was officially done with the conversation.

I turned and started up the stairs.

"What about Brody?" Wes called up after me.

"I'll call him later," I said, then walked down the hall and switched my mind to other things.

Namely, the upcoming party and my deal with Karrie. I found myself wondering what horrible slacker gear she'd show up in this time.

I could hardly wait to find out.

SIX

KARRIE

"I'm starting to think you have a serious problem and need, like, an intervention or something," Ermina said as I laced up my Doc Martins.

"Mina, I'm fine, I swear," I assured her.

"But, you're going to Delta house, right? Dressed like that?" she asked, waving her hand over me in distaste.

I sighed.

"Yes, but, it's not what you think ... I'll explain it all later, I promise, but right now, I have to go or I'm going to be late."

"Would you at least put on some lipstick? Mascara? Please?"

I couldn't help but laugh at her.

"Next time, *promise*," I said as I hurried out the door. She was still frowning at me as I closed it behind me.

Checking my phone, I swore when I saw the time and hurried to my bicycle.

Ten minutes later, I swung into the Delta driveaway, ignored all the stares from well-dressed frat boys and their dowdy-looking dates, and parked my bike on the side of the house.

"Did you just ride here on a bike?"

I finished putting the kickstand down and glanced up to see Ridge leaning on the side of the house.

"Why are you always leaning on walls?" I asked, ignoring his question, because *surely* it was rhetorical.

"It accentuates my length and gives me the chance to watch everyone around me," he answered, pushing off and walking closer.

Not wanting to be overly predictable, I fought back an eye roll and simply scowled at him.

Ridge stopped in front of me, looked me up and down, and smirked.

"What?" I asked, crossing my arms.

"Well, you can keep the Docs, but the rest of it..."

"You told me to dress down so the makeover would look miraculous, or whatever. You should be happy."

"You realize we've only met three times, and you've been wearing that *same* T-shirt every time, don't you?"

I looked down, then shrugged and said, "It's comfortable."

"I hope you at least wash it..."

"Obviously. Just because I like comfort doesn't mean I'm dirty."

Seriously, this fucking guy.

"And, *sweatpants*?" Ridge asked, glaring at said pants. "Sweatpants are okay on Sunday mornings, or when the Dodgers lose the World Series, but I have a feeling this is every day normal attire for you."

"Yeah, well, we don't all have to be Mr. GQ twenty-four seven," I shot back.

"When I look good, I feel good about myself. It's about confidence, and feeling my best. You should try it," he replied, not rising to my bait.

I huffed and felt my shoulders droop.

"I used to, ya know," I said, looking past him, not wanting to meet those eyes. "I used to take care with how I looked, then Drake dumped me out of nowhere and I didn't see the point. After time, this became like my uniform, and eventually, my armor. Dressed this way, I know guys will leave me alone, and honestly, it's easier that way. There's no way I'm putting myself out there again, not after Drake."

"Hey," Ridge said softly, his fingers grasping my chin, urging me to look at him. "Don't give that asshole any more power than he's already had. *Fuck him.* He's in the past, now it's time for you to focus on the future. Let's get this shit over with tonight and then both of our plans will be set in motion. I promise, by the time we're done with you, Drake's going to be *begging* you to take him back."

"As if," I scoffed.

Because, honestly, there was no fucking way Drake could ever make up for what he did to me.

"That's right, and we both know it's right, but Drake doesn't. He's too much of a tool to realize his actions have consequences, but I for one am looking forward to teaching him that lesson."

I smiled up at Ridge.

"Me, too," I replied, then looked around and asked, "He's not going to be here tonight though, right?"

Ridge shook his head.

"Deltas and the girls they're entering into the comp only."

I nodded and couldn't deny I felt relief.

Ridge offered his arm and asked, "Are you ready?"

"As I'll ever be," I replied, tucking my arm around his. "Let's do this."

We rounded the house and started up the stairs.

"Pledge!" Ridge shouted to no one in particular.

An eager-looking blonde guy came running over. "Yes, Sarg?"

"I'll take a beer," Ridge said, before turning his attention to me and asking, "What'll you have?"

"Beer."

"Two beers from my stash," he told the pledge, who nodded before turning and hurrying off.

"Poor guy," I murmured as I watched him go. "I could have gotten my own beer."

"Nah, that's what the pledges are here for. It's like a rite of passage. Believe me, I served plenty of beer back in my day."

We walked inside and I noticed that most everyone had moved into the house. There were guys wearing "pledge" shirts, along with the older, well-dressed guys, who were obviously already part of the frat.

Scattered throughout the rooms were the girls the pledges brought, all looking their worst, with eyes downcast and shoulders hunched, as if they were embarrassed to be seen out in public.

"These girls all know why they're here, right?" I asked Ridge, thinking I was about to *lose my shit* if they were here under false pretenses.

"Yeah, killer, don't worry, even Crush isn't that much of a prick. It's all in good fun," he whispered back, leaning down so that I felt his hot breath against my ear.

A shiver ran through me.

God, he smells good.

"You okay? Cold? I can run up and grab you a hoodie," Ridge offered.

I looked up to see if he was messing with me, but he wasn't even looking at me, he was surveying the room. It appeared his offer had been completely genuine and he hadn't noticed my reaction to him.

Thank goodness. The last thing I needed was for Ridge to think I was even remotely attracted to him. This was a strictly professional relationship. Him smelling good, keeping his room clean, and acting like an occasional gentleman was just a bonus.

"No, I'm good, but thanks."

"Here you go, Sarg, do you need anything else?"

The pledge was back.

I accepted the bottle of Stella and said, "Thanks," to the pledge, before glancing up at Ridge and saying, "*Fancy.*"

"Only the best, baby," Ridge said with a wink.

Annnnd ... we're back to eye-rolling.

SEVEN
RIDGE

"Welcome, welcome. I'm ready to get started," Crush called, causing everyone to look to where he was standing, on top of the ledge in front of the fireplace in the common room. "I'd like to say thanks to all the ladies who agreed to help these poor, insignificant pledges. Their mission is to turn you all into the hottest girls on campus in time for the big Delta Homecoming party."

Crush paused and looked around the room. I don't know if he thought he had the room eating out of the palm of his hands or what, but while the pledges looked scared, the girls looked kinda pissed.

"Tonight, I will personally meet each and every one of you and either approve or disapprove of the pledges' choice. If I approve, we'll see you back here Homecoming night; if I disapprove, that pledge is out of the running. The pledge who wins gets fifty points, *and* the opportunity to have a private dinner with the board."

Karrie poked my shoulder, so I leaned down.

"What are the points for?" she whispered in my ear.

"The pledges earn points to become members," I replied.

"And, what's the benefit of a dinner with the board?"

I glanced at her, saw she was seriously curious, and said, "It gives them the opportunity to talk to us individually ... privately, and give us more insight into who they are as a person, rather than just a pledge. It's hard to give individual attention to each pledge, and they usually don't get that chance until we've already gone through two rounds of weeding them out."

"Hmmm," Karrie murmured, then asked, "But, what's in it for the girls?"

"What's in it for you, you may be asking," Crush began, and I stood back up, wondering what his answer would be. "Well, other than having access to the Deltas and our house over the next few weeks during the competition, the winning girl will have an open invite to every Delta event during her career here at U of M."

I glanced down to see Karrie's reaction and chuckled when she gave me a dry stare.

"To give you an idea of what I'm looking for," Crush continued. "Bella..."

He held his hand out and Bella, his fuck buddy, came out of the kitchen and started moving through the crowd. The pledges and their girls parted, all eyes on Bella as she strutted toward Crush.

Wearing stilettos, a skin-tight leather dress, and what I'd bet a Benjamin was a wig, Bella placed her hand in his and let him pull her up onto his makeshift stage.

When she turned and faced the crowd, there was an audible gasp.

Yeah, sure, Bella was gorgeous, but she was seventy-five percent fake and one-hundred percent a raging bitch.

Not exactly who the young girls on campus should aspire to be.

"This is what a winner looks like," Crush said with a dumbass grin.

"What a dipshit," Karrie muttered and I grinned down at her.

"Right?" I agreed.

"So, go forth ... eat, drink, and get ready for my inspection," Crush said, hopping down off the stage and leaving Bella on display.

God, what a fucking douche.

"You hungry?" I asked Karrie. "There's some pizza and chips and stuff in the kitchen."

She lifted a shoulder and replied, "I can always eat."

I put my hand on the small of her back and led her to the kitchen.

Once inside, I rounded the counter and grabbed some paper plates. Luckily, no one else had come in search of food yet; they were probably all anxiously awaiting Crush's decision.

I handed Karrie a plate and noticed her watching me warily.

"What?" I asked, opening pizza boxes until I found a supreme.

"So, are we dating now?"

She put air quotes over *dating*.

I looked toward the door to make sure no one was coming before turning back to her and saying, "I figured we'd ease into it. We'll be spending time with each other as we work on your makeover, and eventually we'll start incorporating PDA and I'll drop hints that we're dating."

Karrie grabbed a pepperoni and sausage slice and jumped up on the counter to sit.

"I've been wondering," she began, her gaze on me pensive. "If we just need to convince your mom that we're dating over Thanksgiving, why do we need to pretend over the next few months? Here? Can't we save it for the trip?"

I shook my head.

"My brother's a pledge. I need to start the ruse here so he gets wind of it and tells our mom; that way, it'll be more believable when I take you home. Since Wes goes to school here and's a pledge, he would know if I was seriously dating someone."

"We're going to lie to your brother?" she asked, not looking happy about it.

"Yeah, at least until after Thanksgiving," I told her. "I'll come clean once we get back and have officially *broken up*. Wes is a total mama's boy. I need him to believe we're together so that *she'll* believe we're together."

"What are you talking about?"

I shifted to see my brother walking into the kitchen, a petite girl with long black hair and a scowl following behind him.

"Nothing you need to concern yourself with, *pledge*," I replied, hoping he hadn't heard what Karrie and I'd been discussing. "How's it going? You guys have your meet with Crush yet?"

"Guy's a total dick," the raven-haired chick scoffed.

"That he is," I agreed. "Hi, I'm Ridge, Sergeant at Arms, and this rude asshole's older brother."

"Trixie," she replied, shaking my offered hand.

"And, this is Karrie, my date for the evening," I said, turning to include Karrie, who was watching us from her perch. "Karrie, my brother, Wes, and his offering for the night, Trixie."

"Hey, Karrie, it's nice to meet you," Wes said, finally remembering his manners and moving to take her hand in his.

His eyes were twinkling and he held her hand for a bit longer than necessary, so I walked over to him and pulled him away.

"Hands off my date," I told him, needing to establish boundaries, and interest, right off the bat if he was ever going to believe Karrie and I were dating by Thanksgiving.

I wasn't exactly known for dating seriously and had never taken anyone home to *meet the parents.*

Wes looked up at me, surprise evident on his face, and held up his hands in surrender.

"You got it," he replied, and backed away.

"Nice to meet you, Wes ... Trixie," Karrie said, placing her plate next to her with only the crust left.

"You're not going to eat the crust?" I asked her.

She shook her head. "No, I don't like it. Too much dough."

"That's sacrilege. You can't call yourself a pizza connoisseur and not eat the crust."

"Good thing I don't call myself that, then," Karrie said as she hopped down. "Do we need to go in and meet Crush so we can get his approval?

She said *Crush* with a sneer that I enjoyed.

"*Fuck that,*" I replied. "I'm not part of the competition, so Crush has zero say in you, me, or how we decide to make you over."

"Okay," Karrie said, wiping her hands with a napkin. "What should we do then?"

"Beer pong?" I suggested.

She grinned at me and replied, "You're on."

EIGHT
KARRIE

I caught a glance of myself in the mirror while I washed my hands, and a giggle escaped my lips.

My flannel shirt was now tied around the waist of my cutoff sweats, so you could see all of the writing on my favorite T-shirt, which showcased different lyrics from Thirty Seconds to Mars songs. Paired with my Docs and completely messy up-do, I looked totally grunge.

Like I'd walked right out of a portal from the nineties.

I swear, I'd seen Crush's lip curl up when he saw me and Ridge playing beer pong. Which, by the way, Ridge obviously had a lot of experience in, because I was totally smashed and he seemed no worse for the wear.

Wes, on the other hand, had passed out in the corner of the room. Trixie had looked at him with contempt and gone home with a few of the other girls.

Still giggling, I swung open the bathroom door to see Ridge leaning against the wall, arms crossed, eyes on me.

"You're leaning again," I told him, trying not to trip over my feet as I stepped into the hall.

"What's so funny?" he asked, ignoring my observation and taking me by the arm to help me stay upright.

"Nothin', just how rad you look."

"Rad, huh?"

"Yup," I said, popping the *p*.

"Do you want me to take you home, or would you rather go up to my room and crash here?"

I swung my head toward him, *much too quickly*, and asked, "Is it safe?"

"Safe? What, to go to my room?" he asked, pulling me against him when I started to waiver.

"Yeah, you're not gonna try any funny business, right?"

Ridge scoffed.

"I don't make a habit of pawing at wasted girls, even if they look like members of the Nirvana fan club."

"Good one," I said, as he pointed me toward the stairs. "Are you sure there isn't some hot chick in stilettos waiting to warm your bed?"

"Jealous?" he asked.

I tried to guffaw, but it came out somewhere between a snort and a burp.

"You gonna be sick?" Ridge asked, moving us faster.

"Your insinuation that I'd be jealous of *you* makes me sick, but physically ... no."

"Okay, well, let me know if you do feel like puking, I have a bathroom off of my room, and I'd rather you make it to the toilet, than vomit on my bed."

"Will do, Captain," I said, giving him a jaunty salute.

Ridge shook his head and propped me up against the wall while he unlocked his door.

"You lock it?" I asked, letting my head fall back.

"Not always, but during parties, definitely."

"Hmmm, I don't remember it being locked last time I was up here."

He looked at me with annoyance.

"Just an observation," I said with a wave of my hand. "No need to get your panties in a bunch."

Ridge just sighed. "Come on, killer, let's get you inside before you fall over."

He led me to the bed and I laid back on it with a happy squeal.

"Mmm, soft."

"Here, take these."

I opened one eye to see Ridge standing over me with one hand out and the other holding a Gatorade.

Sitting up, I took the pills he offered and the blue drink. Before popping them in my mouth, I looked closer at the pills, saw they said Motrin on them, and took them.

"Thanks."

"Drink all the Gatorade," Ridge ordered.

"*Yes, sir.*"

Ridge got some clothes out of his dresser and disappeared into the bathroom while I downed the rest of the drink. Once it was done, I set the empty bottle on the side table and laid back down on the bed.

"Is Wes your only brother?" I asked, then realized the last time I'd seen him was in the beer pong room. "Hey, is he going to be okay? Did you leave him in the corner?"

The door opened and Ridge stepped out wearing basketball shorts and a plain white tee.

"Don't worry, a couple of the pledges had to stay sober to make sure the rest of them got home safe. Wes'll be fine. And, no, our youngest brother's Brody. He's a senior in high school, but he'll be coming to U of M next year."

"Wow, all of you at the same school. That's pretty cool ... I mean, as long as you all like each other."

"Yeah, we get along, it'll be good for Brody to get away," Ridge said, opening his drawer again and holding up a T-shirt. "You wanna put this on? It's probably more comfortable than that."

I looked down and saw my Docs were perched on his bed and quickly swung my feet to the floor.

"Sorry," I mumbled, placing my hands on either side of me to steady myself on the bed.

"Here, let me help."

Ridge crouched before me and started unlacing my boots.

"I didn't think you'd be this nice," I told him softly, enjoying the way his dark hair fell over his forehead.

"Don't be fooled, I can be a total dick," Ridge said, his blue eyes intense when he met my gaze. "But, you and I, we're a team now, we need to have each other's backs."

I started to nod, but the room started spinning, so I stopped.

Once my boots were off, I scooted back up on the bed and laid my head on his soft, yet firm pillow.

"What about you?" Ridge asked as he crawled in beside me. "Do you have any brothers or sisters?"

Turning on my side, I tucked my hands under my cheeks and looked at him.

"I do ... My mom and dad met when I was like two, at college. He was a baseball player and she was working her way through school and raising me. Eventually they got married, and now I have a younger brother, Carter." I paused, thinking about my family and how much I missed them.

"So, he's your stepdad?"

"Yeah, Judd's my stepdad, but really the only father I've ever known. Initially, my real dad, Tucker, didn't want anything to do with having a kid. He and my mom were just a hookup and he had dreams of playing professional baseball, which he did. About five years ago, he settled down and got married and realized what an ass he'd been. He contacted my mom and asked if we could meet. She left it up to me."

"So, both Judd and your dad were ballplayers?"

"Mmm-hmmm, on the same team. I guess they were even friends, until Judd found out Tucker was a deadbeat dad. They hadn't talked to each other either, until five years ago."

"What did you decide? Did you give him a shot?"

"Yeah," I said, trying to cover a yawn. "I met him and his wife, Claire, and once they had my little sister, Evelyn, I started spending more time with them. Now we're a big, crazy, dysfunctional family."

"Sounds cool," Ridge said. "My brothers and I just recently found out we have three sisters, who are all older than us. My dad was a deadbeat too, and didn't have anything to do with them once he left their mom for ours. So, I have a crazy dysfunctional family, too."

"Huh, who would've thought?"

"What?"

"That we actually have something in common," I joked, and then I couldn't fight it anymore, and fell asleep.

NINE
RIDGE

I woke up quickly, going from dead-ass asleep to wide awake in seconds, just like I did every morning. And, just like every morning, my dick was hard. This time, however, it was cozied up to something very soft and supple.

Karrie's ass.

Despite my cock's protest, I rolled over and out of bed, being as quiet and speedy as possible, so as not to wake my partner in crime and give her more ammunition against me.

Because, seriously, morning wood was as common as breathing, and had nothing to do with how good Karrie's hair smelled, or how deliciously curved her ass was. It was simply how the male body worked ... it didn't mean anything.

That was my mantra as I locked myself in the bathroom, jumped in the shower, and jacked off.

If Karrie popped in my mind a couple times, or twenty, it was only because I just spent the night next to her, not because I thought she was hot.

Once I was clean and no longer ruled by my hard-on, I wrapped a towel around my waist and went back into my room to get dressed.

And, I'm stiff again.

Karrie was sitting up against my headboard, her curly hair a riot around her face, which was soft with sleep.

Her lips were full and pouty, and I instantly imagined them wrapped around my dick.

Fuck.

"Morning," she said with a smile, her voice low and rough.

That isn't helping.

"Good morning," I managed, grateful that I had big extra-long and thick towels, so there was no evidence of my traitorous desire. "Feeling okay?"

I turned my back on her as I pulled my boxers out of the drawer, then moved to the closet and went inside.

"Yeah, great actually. Your Gatorade trick worked wonders."

"Good," I called out through the half-closed door as I got dressed.

"Who knew you were so smart?" she asked with a smirk when I came out.

"I did," I retorted, and was pleased when she laughed.

Why that pleased me, I had no idea.

I need to shake this shit off.

"What's your schedule look like today?" I asked.

"Free morning and one class this afternoon. I tried to get all of my classes on the same days, but the teacher I wanted for accounting only had one class available, so I had to take it. Why?"

"I thought we could get a jump on things and go shopping, but if you're busy..."

"My class is over at three, we could go after," Karrie suggested.

"That works for me, where should I pick you up?"

"My apartment at three thirty? That would give me the chance to drop my stuff off. I can text you the address."

"Sounds good," I replied as I shoved my books into my backpack and threw it over my shoulder.

"Are you leaving?" she asked.

"Yeah, I have class. You don't have to hurry out, but I wouldn't spend too much time down in the common rooms, there's no telling what you'll see or hear," I warned her. "I have some stuff in my mini fridge, and snacks in that cabinet. Help yourself."

"Okay, thanks," Karrie said, but her expression conveyed her discomfort. "See you later."

"Will you be okay? Do you need me to wait and walk you out?" I asked, looking at my phone and seeing I only had ten minutes to get to class.

"No, I'm a big girl, I'll be fine," she said, lifting her chin.

I nodded, taking her at her word.

"Later."

I hurried down the stairs, said, "Hey," to the pledge who was cleaning up, and rushed to my car.

Once I found a parking spot and did a light jog to my building, I made it to class with one minute to spare.

I was about to grab the seat in the back left corner that I'd claimed as mine, when I saw Drake standing by the door talking to a couple teammates, and redirected myself.

"Hey, asshole," I said as I walked up to them, lifting my chin at the other guys and adding, "Connor, Marcus."

Connor and Marcus said hi, but Drake just sneered.

"I wanted to thank you for being such a dick. Looks like you inadvertently did me a favor," I told him with a smirk.

"Oh yeah, how so?" he asked, taking the bait.

Dude was so fucking predictable.

"By being a dumbass and letting Karrie go..."

Drake looked me up and down, so I stood a little straighter, making sure he had to look up at me to finish his perusal.

"Karrie wouldn't touch you with a ten-foot pole, preppy."

"That's funny, cause I'm pretty sure I have a date with her tonight," I replied, leaning in close to get in his face.

"Bullshit," he retorted, but he no longer looked sure.

I grinned.

"Sorry, but it's true," I said, making sure he saw the intent in my eyes. "And, I hate to break it to you, but when I left Delta, she was still warming my bed."

Drake's eyes widened and his lips thinned.

"I just love the smell of honey and cinnamon, don't you?"

That did it. Describing the smell of her hair was all he needed to believe Karrie and I had spent the night together.

"Later, fuckwad," I said with a laugh, then spun round and went to find my seat.

TEN
KARRIE

It felt like the walk of shame, even though I hadn't done anything to feel ashamed of.

Not that I thought having sex, one-night stands, or spending the night with a guy you had a mutually beneficial understanding with was anything to be ashamed of. But, walking through Delta that morning after sleeping in Ridge's room, I'd been very unsettled at the thought of anyone seeing me.

I didn't want to be seen as a *Delta Groupie*, or one of Ridge's randoms.

I wasn't sure why it mattered to me, but it did.

Luckily, I made it out with only one pledge seeing me, and he'd looked like he was more afraid of me than I was of him.

Feeling surprisingly chipper, considering how much I drank last night, I hopped on my bike and pedaled home, enjoying the feel of the sun on my skin as I navigated the streets.

There were students everywhere. Some headed to class, others piling out of the coffee shop, and I smiled as I realized for the first time since Drake broke up with me, that I was happy and excited to see what the day would bring.

After I locked up my bike, I hurried upstairs and into my

apartment, throwing open the door and calling *Good morning* to Mina.

"What's so good about it? Where have you been? Are those yesterday's clothes? Spill!"

I laughed as I turned to look at my best friend, who was eating cereal at the counter.

"Don't get excited, nothing happened ... but I spent the night at Delta," I told her, feeling an odd thrill at the memory of falling asleep next to Ridge.

"*Shut the front door,*" Mina cried, doing a little high step in place. "With Ridge?"

"Yes, but like I said, nothing happened. We just hung out, played some beer pong, and then he let me sleep it off in his room," I told her.

I really wanted to spill all ... the makeover, the fake dating, etc... but since Ridge wanted to keep this secret from everyone, including his own brother, I didn't know how he'd feel about me letting Mina in on it.

"In his bed?" she asked gleefully.

"Yes."

"With him in it?"

I nodded.

"But nothing happened?" Mina pressed. "No accidental touches or inadvertent kisses? Tell me you at least grazed his dick."

I couldn't help but laugh.

"Well, let's just say I did feel a wakeup call on my ass this morning," I admitted.

"And? Was it a big wakeup call, or just a little guy?"

"Oh, it was substantial."

"I knew it. Dude's big all over, it would be depressing if the girth didn't match the stature, if you get my drift," she said wryly.

"He's not getting complaints in the girth department, I can assure you of that."

"Mmmmm," Mina said, shaking her head. "Did you at least wiggle up against it?"

"No, I pretended to be asleep."

"What a wasted opportunity," she chided.

"I didn't want to complicate things," I told her truthfully, even though I knew we were about to ramp up our makeover game, and with the way Mina was acting, she was going to fall for it hook, line, and sinker.

I needed to talk to Ridge and see if he'd be okay with me telling Mina the truth. I didn't want to lie to her, especially not when she was so excited about even the possibility of me and Ridge.

"Girl, you got a man that fine, hard and ready to go, you do whatever you can to get yourself some. You could have started your day off with an orgasm. When's the last time that happened?"

"Um..."

"Exactly. Ridge is hot as fuck, plus, you could throw that shit in Drake's face."

I nodded, since that was the whole reason I agreed to Ridge's crazy scheme in the first place. Drake had always been jealous, and even though he'd apparently cheated on me repeatedly and moved on, I knew he still wouldn't like the idea of *me* moving on with someone else.

Especially Ridge.

"Well, I am seeing Ridge tonight, so we'll see what happens."

Mina's eyes widened and she threw a fist in the air.

"Yes! This is the best news I've heard all day. Now, please tell me that you're finally going to change your clothes and do something with your hair," she said, curling her lip as she looked me over. "You need to show Ridge that you're more than sweats and a messy bun."

"Actually, he's taking me shopping ... for clothes."

"Seriously? Did he lose a bet or something?"

"It was actually his idea," I told her.

"It's because of that shirt, isn't it? He thinks you're a poor student with no fashion sense and he's taking pity on you."

I slapped her on the arm.

"*Ouch*."

"That's not true," I argued, even though it probably was.

Mina gave me a look that said, *it absolutely is true*, and said, "Just promise me you'll put some effort in so Ridge can see how you look when you're not sad and depressed Karrie who doesn't give a shit."

"I promise," I told her.

"Good, now promise that you'll try to get to first base ... maybe second."

"No," I said with a laugh, "we're going out as friends."

"Wear that sundress you have, with the little flowers and tight bodice. Ridge will be begging to round the bases with you."

"*Mina...*"

"No, Karrie, you deserve this. You deserve to have some fun after what that fuck did to you and Ridge looks like he'd be an amusement park full of fun."

ELEVEN
RIDGE

I jogged up the stairs to Karrie's apartment and knocked.

I felt an anticipation I couldn't quite explain, since I was just picking her up to go shopping, which wasn't very exciting.

Maybe it was because I wanted to tell her about my run-in with Drake, or see if memory served and she looked as hot as she had in my bed that morning. Hell, maybe I just wanted to spend more time with her again.

It was weird, but I wasn't going to dwell on my feelings. I was simply going to go with it and see what happened.

My greeting of, "*Hey,*" was on my lips as the door opened, but it fell off when I got a good look at Karrie.

Her blonde hair framed her face with soft curls, looking more controlled than I'd ever seen it. Her face was done up tastefully in neutral tones, and her body was encased in a very flattering, form-fitting dress that showed off her toned body.

The girl looked thick in all the right ways, and utterly gorgeous.

I blinked and looked behind her, as if searching for the T-shirt-wearing girl who threw her hair up and walked around with a *no fucks given* attitude.

"Hi," Karrie's voice said from the bombshell's mouth, and I blinked my focus back on her.

"Hey," I said again, not sure if I'd actually said it initially or not, even though I probably sounded like an idiot.

She gave me a confused smile and stepped aside.

"So you want to come in?"

I looked over her shoulder again, into the living room with throw pillows and blankets galore, and shook my head.

"Nah, we'd better head out."

"Sounds good, let me grab my bag," Karrie said, leaving me alone in the doorway while I tried to gather my wits.

I mean, I'd chosen her because I figured she'd clean up nice, but this was ridiculous. My dick was hard and I kept seeing flashes of her full pink-stained lips, and I knew if I didn't get my shit together I'd wind up saying or doing something I'd regret.

Remember your deal, I told myself mentally, turning from the doorway and closing my eyes as I tried to soften my hard-on.

"Ready," I heard Karrie say behind me, the door clicking shut.

"Great, let's go," I replied, not turning to look at her again, but instead crossing to the stairs and hurrying down them.

I was quiet as we got in my car and I turned us toward the mall.

"Is everything okay?" Karrie asked softly, her tone conveying her nerves.

"Yup," I said, and it was, now that I had my hormones under control. "You have any issues at the house this morning?"

My voice must have sounded normal, because the nerves were gone when she answered, "Nope, none at all. But, when I got home wearing yesterday's clothes, I did get shit from Mina, which made me wonder ... can I tell her about our deal, or is she supposed to think we're dating for real? I didn't mention anything, because I wasn't sure and wanted to talk to you about it first."

I shifted to look at her, before turning my attention back to the road as I pulled into the parking garage.

"I'd rather we keep the fact that it's all bullshit to ourselves," I told her, somewhat harshly.

"O-kay," Karrie said slowly, and I could feel her eyes on my face. "Are you all right?"

Once I was parked, I turned in my seat and said, "Yeah, and, not to be a dick, but I was clear about wanting our deal to be kept a secret. It doesn't take long for rumors to spread on campus, and if this was going to work, *for both of us*, we need people to believe what started as a frat house game turned into a real relationship. That won't happen if we started letting people in on the secret."

"Okay, and that's fine. I didn't tell her anything because it apparently wasn't clear to me, and I wanted to make sure. And, full disclosure, you *are* being a dick."

Before I could respond, Karrie hopped out and shut the door behind her with a bang.

"*Shit*," I exclaimed, as I hurried after her calling, "*Karrie...*"

I tried not to notice how good her ass looked in that dress, and failed.

"Look, Karrie, wait up, okay?"

I reached out and put my hand on her arm, but when she shot a glare at me, I let her go.

"Hey, I'm sorry."

Karrie stopped walking and let me catch up with arms crossed and foot tapping.

"You're right, I was being a dick."

"You've been weird since you picked me up."

I nodded, secretly liking the fact that she called me on my shit. "You're right, I've been feeling off, and I took it out on you."

"Did something happen?"

I shook my head.

"No, I don't know what crawled up my ass," I lied, but I wasn't about to tell her I couldn't handle being around *smokin' hot Karrie*. "Today was actually a good day ... I had a run-in with Drake earlier."

"Really? What happened?"

"Well, I may have insinuated that we're *together* together. I told him we're going on a date tonight, and that I'd left you in my bed this morning."

Her mouth formed a surprised "O," which brought more dirty thoughts to my mind.

"You didn't." Karrie smacked me on the arm.

"Yeah, I did. The whole point is for him to see you moving on, right? Well, I helped that along this morning."

"Was he pissed?" she asked hopefully.

"Totally jealous," I assured her with a grin.

A movement out of the corner of my eye caught my attention, and I glanced over to see the man himself glaring at us from the entrance to the food court.

Taking a step closer, I tipped my lips up in a cocky grin and lowered my voice.

"What are you doing?" Karrie asked, watching me get closer, eyes wary.

"Showtime," I whispered. "He's watching us right now."

"Who, Drake?" she asked, and I could see it was killing her not to look around.

"Yup. You ready?"

"For what?" Karrie asked, those big blue eyes wide as they looked up at me.

I stepped closer, so close the material of her dress brushed against my legs.

"Our first kiss."

Her lips parted at my words, and when she didn't audibly protest, I brought one hand up to delve into her curls while the other settled on the curve of her hip.

"Be convincing."

I wasn't sure if I was talking to her, or to myself, but I needn't have bothered. The second our lips touched the heat between us was palpable.

TWELVE

KARRIE

There was a squeak of surprise, followed by a moan, both of which I think came from me, but I was too swept up to care.

Because ... Oh. My. God. I'm kissing Ridge and it is freaking amazing.

His palm on my hip felt like a brand, hot and heavy and searing through my dress. Then, there was the hand that was currently fisted in my hair, tugging just enough so that I knew it was there, and inexplicably driving me over the edge.

Drake had never squeezed, pulled, or bit anything, and as Ridge's teeth grazed my lower lip, I found all three actions really, *really* got my engines revved.

In fact, I lost all awareness of our surroundings and was seconds away from climbing him like the rope in gym class when he released me and stepped away.

"*Gah,*" was the sound that came out of my mouth as I reached blindly for him, wanting to pull him back.

Luckily, his eyes were closed and it looked like he was also struggling for composure, so he didn't see my embarrassing move or hear me struggling to regain the ability to breathe normally.

You'd think I'd never been kissed before, but I guess the take home from this moment for me, was that I'd never been so caught up in a kiss, in feeling every pulse point in my body, that I'd been reduced to a quivering mass of need within seconds.

Jesus, Ridge is potent.

I started reciting the phonetic alphabet in my head to calm my racing heart and get back to normal so I could face Ridge as a perfectly rational woman when he was done reciting whatever mantra he used to calm the raging boner in his shorts.

Seriously, it was impressive, and I had to force myself to avert my gaze and focus on the alphabet, because my body was screaming for me to tackle him.

After a few minutes of working on our individual techniques, Ridge and I gave each other shaky smiles and wordlessly started into the mall.

We were crossing the entrance to the food court when I remembered what had started the kiss and surveyed our surroundings for the first time.

"I don't see him."

"Who?" Ridge asked, trying to adjust himself inconspicuously.

"Drake."

"Probably ran off crying..."

"Yeah, right," I muttered, even as the terrible side of me secretly hoped it was true. "So, where to first?"

"This way," Ridge replied, taking me by the arm and leading me through the food court and past all the stores I usually shopped in.

"Whoa," I said, putting on the breaks when he stopped in front of Gucci.

"What?"

"I'm not going in there," I said, digging in my heels when he tried to tug me.

"Why the hell not?"

"Because, I'm not a Gucci girl."

"Well, I'm a Gucci guy, and I'm the one doing the makeover, so ... move."

I shook my head and Ridge let out an exasperated breath.

"Ridge, I'm a broke college student," I explained. "And, yes, you're footing this makeover bill, but it still needs to be clothes that I'll actually wear. I'm not going anywhere in a four-hundred-dollar T-shirt."

"Where do you want to go, *the fucking Gap*?"

I rolled my eyes at him, cause, seriously?

"No, I don't want to go to *The Gap*. Look, I know you think because we're about to be *dating*," I said, using air quotes, "that you need me to look like the kind of bougie chick you'd have on your arm, and I get that. But, I also have to be me. There are two sides to this deal, remember? And, no one who knows me would believe that I woke up this morning, and your dick was *so good*, that I suddenly morphed into a Gucci-wearing diva."

Ridge looked at me for a moment before sighing.

"Well, for one, my dick *is* that good, but I get your point. Where is it you want to go?" he asked. "And, don't say Hot Topic or some such nonsense, there has to be a place that is a mix of the two of us. There's no way I'm taking you to Thanksgiving wearing a *Sonic the Hedgehog* T-shirt."

"Hey, Sonic's coming back," I joked, taking his hand in mine and leading him away from the God-awful expensive part of the mall.

I took him to a store that, although I couldn't afford myself, I really liked. It was a mix of name brands and high-end stuff for Ridge, but cool, fun surfer/skater stuff that I liked. The perfect compromise.

"I can work with this," Ridge managed as I led him inside.

We split up and started looking at clothes, each of us choosing items and putting them in a dressing room for me to try on. When I had more clothes waiting than I had in my closet, I left Ridge sitting in a wingback chair while I went to start trying them on.

"You have to show me," Ridge called out once I was behind the closed door.

"Only if I like it!" I yelled back.

I thought I heard him mutter, *fine*, but couldn't be sure.

After a few definite *nopes*, I put on a sweet white cropped shirt with bell sleeves and a light denim mini skirt, and declared it a winner.

I walked out to where Ridge was waiting, but he was so engrossed on whatever he was watching on his phone that he didn't look up.

I cleared my throat.

Ridge looked up slowly, and I caught the slight widening of his eyes, which made me grin.

"What do you think?" I asked, turning in a circle.

"Not quite Thanksgiving wear, but ... *schwing*!"

I barked out a laugh.

"Did you just make a *Wayne's World* reference?"

"Yeah, why?"

"I just didn't think you had it in you," I joked.

"When we were kids, my brothers and I would escape to the movie theater downstairs and watch nineties movies. Our nanny was obsessed, and she got us into them."

"Did you just say you had a movie theater in your house *and* a nanny?"

Ridge shrugged one shoulder. "Yeah, Karrie, what part of *my family is rich* don't you understand?"

Not appreciating his tone, I put my hand on my hip and glared at him.

"I don't know, Ridge *McRitcherson*, maybe when you don't grow up with theaters, nannies, and closets full of Gucci, it's hard to comprehend."

"McRitcherson?" he asked with a grin.

"Yup, it's what I'm calling you now."

"Please, don't."

"Anyway, I like this outfit, so it's going in the *keep* pile."

"Agreed."

"And, in spite of that other stuff," I said with a wave of my hand. "I like that you make *Wayne's World* references. In fact, it may be my favorite thing about you."

"Yeah?" he asked.

"Yup."

"You know, most of the people we know would think *Wayne's World* is anything but cool," Ridge said.

This time, I shrugged and said, "Well, most people we know are idiots," before spinning and heading back to try on more clothes.

THIRTEEN
RIDGE

I was sitting there, chuckling and shaking my head, when I felt someone come up next to me and pat me on the arm.

I looked up and to my right to see Caitlyn, one of the Delta groupies, standing there with an armful of clothes and a smile.

"Hey, Ridge, how's it going?" she asked.

My eyes flitted to the closed dressing room door, before coming back to rest on Caitlyn. We'd hooked up a couple times, but when she'd tried to move us toward a relationship, I'd quickly put a stop to it.

Not only did I not do relationships, but Caitlyn was almost as entitled as I was, and I needed someone who was a little more grounded. Who'd put me in my place and not let me walk all over them. Someone who'd call me on my shit and not get offended when I called them on theirs.

A mental picture of Karrie popped in my head, but I ignored it. Karrie and I would never work. First of all, she was hung up on her asshole ex, and second of all, she was simply a means to an end.

Not at all girlfriend material.

Guilt slammed through me at that stray thought, but I ignored it and answered the girl hovering over me.

"Can't complain," I answered, intentionally not continuing the conversation in hopes that she'd get the hint and leave me alone.

I looked back down at my phone.

"I heard Delta's planning a rager for after Homecoming ... something about making over girls into the perfect Delta groupies. Crush should have asked me to come be an example, not Bella. I've been hanging with Deltas for the last four years," she continued with a pout.

I sighed and brought my gaze back up to her face.

"It was Crush's deal, Caitlyn, I'm not involved in his shit."

She smirked and replied, "That's not what I heard. Word on the street is you picked a girl for a makeover, too. Drake's girl."

"Word on the street?" I scoffed, standing up and stretching, and shooting her a bored expression. "Your source is wrong. Karrie is more to me than a game Crush is playing with the rushes. And, she's not Drake's girl ... She's mine."

Just then, the changing room door swung open, and Karrie walked out wearing a tight-fitting tube dress that showed off her curves, leaving little to the imagination. By the sweet grin on her face, and the way she crossed to me and put her arm around my waist, tucking into my side, I knew she'd heard everything Caitlyn and I had said.

"Hey, babe," she cooed, pulling me tight. "I hope I'm not taking too long."

I looked down at her upturned face and felt my heart accelerate.

"You're worth the wait," I said softly, my eyes falling to her lips as I remembered our kiss.

"Aww, you're so sweet," Karrie said, turning her attention to Caitlyn and repeating, "Isn't he *so* sweet?"

"The sweetest," Caitlyn replied, her tone implying I was anything but.

"And you are?" Karrie asked, one hand resting on my abs, causing me to flex.

"Caitlyn."

"Hi, Caitlyn, I'm Karrie, Ridge's girlfriend."

I would have laughed at the shocked look on Caitlyn's face, but I was too busy enjoying the feel of Karrie's hand on me. I found myself wishing there was no barrier between that hand and my bare skin.

Caitlyn recovered and let out a disbelieving laugh.

"Ridge doesn't date," she said, like she knew the first fucking thing about me.

"Well, that's obviously not true."

Caitlyn looked to me, as if expecting me to prove her right and call Karrie a liar.

Instead I wrapped my arms around her and kissed the top of her head.

"I never saw a reason to date, then I met Karrie."

Caitlyn's eyes narrowed, and I knew she was pissed, like I'd just said she wasn't good enough for me.

Which, honestly, was true.

I looked at her pointedly, daring her to say something else, but instead she simply huffed and threw the clothes she'd been holding on the ground.

When she spun on her heel and stormed off, Karrie called after her, "You can't just leave the clothes like that." But Caitlyn didn't stop, she stormed out of the store.

"What an asshole," Karrie said, untangling herself from me and putting distance between us.

I missed her warmth immediately, and it took a minute before it registered that she was bending over and picking up Caitlyn's discarded clothes.

"You don't have to do that. There are employees..."

Karrie raised her head and glared at me, giving me the perfect view of her breasts, which I took a moment to appreciate.

"They shouldn't have to," she argued.

"Neither should you," I replied, moving to help her.

Once the clothes were hanging in an open dressing room, Karrie turned to me and said, "Guess we're out of the closet."

I nodded in agreement.

"Yup. Between Drake and Caitlyn, the news will be all over Greek row and the sports complex by dinner."

"What do you think of this one?" she asked, waving her hand across her body.

"Fucking fantastic," I replied without hesitation. "But not Thanksgiving attire."

"Don't worry, I have the perfect dress in there for Thanksgiving, I'll try on next. And, this will go in the keep pile."

I threw my thanks up to God before asking, "What are you thinking for dinner? I'm getting hungry."

"The food court's right there, we can hit it up after I'm done."

"The food court?" I asked, curling my lip. "I was hoping for a restaurant ... you know, with service and actual dishes."

Karrie gave an exaggerated eyeroll that had me biting back a smile.

"Don't tell me you've never eaten in the food court."

"Why would I?"

"Jeez, what kind of college student are you? Are you even getting the college experience?"

I looked up and tapped my mouth like I was thinking about it, before saying, "The amount of alcohol and pussy I've consumed say *yes*."

"Ugh," Karrie moaned, slapping me on the arm. "You're so

gross. Let's save the restaurant with its fancy plates for next time. Tonight, you're getting a Philly cheesesteak and greasy fries from the food court. My treat."

I shook my head.

"I'm the bankroll in this relationship, remember?"

"Don't worry, I'll let you foot the bill for the clothes, but I'm paying for dinner. I need to feel like I'm contributing something to this relationship. I was raised to pay my own way."

I could tell by her expression that she was serious, and pride was an emotion I could understand, so I nodded in agreement, then lifted my chin toward her dressing room.

"Fine, now go finish trying this stuff on before my stomach eats itself."

Karrie rolled her eyes again and muttered, "So dramatic."

And, when I went back to my uncomfortable chair, I couldn't help but shake my head and grin.

FOURTEEN
KARRIE

I ignored the rush of pleasure I got from watching Ridge consume his Philly with gusto.

Something about watching a man enjoy a meal ... no, I hadn't made it, but it was my idea to come here, and I'd pushed him into trying something different. The fact that he was enjoying it did something funny to my insides.

I was afraid I was starting to like Ridge too much.

Sure, he was a pig, rich and pretty conceited, and he didn't live in the same world I did, but there was something about him. He was funny, charming, and handsome as hell. And, although he could be an asshole, he wasn't a dick, and had so far treated me with respect.

Plus, there was a chemistry between us that I'd never felt with anyone before. It was almost like we'd known each other all of our lives, instead of a couple weeks. With Ridge things were easy.

He was straightforward and honest. I liked that I never had to wonder what he was thinking.

"Mmm," Ridge grunted as he finished off his sandwich.

"Good?" I asked with a laugh, since he'd obviously

enjoyed it.

"So good ... Who knew the food court had such delicious offerings?" he asked incredulously, which made me start laughing harder. "What's so funny?"

I tried to stem my laughter and not choke on the fry I'd been chewing.

When I could talk, and no longer had food in my mouth, I replied, "I've never seen someone get so excited about the food court before."

"Yeah, well I've never seen anyone so excited about a pair of shoes before," Ridge replied dryly.

I flushed.

Ridge had bought me a pair of Sonia Rykiel wedge sandals to go with my Thanksgiving dress. They were gorgeous and crazy expensive. A purchase I had never and would never make for myself, but I think I'd had a mini orgasm when I'd tried them on.

Ridge had whipped out his AMEX and bought them immediately.

"Touché," I replied, still feeling guilty over how much money he'd spent on me.

"Hey," Ridge called, leaning over the table toward me as he reached for my hand. "Don't. We already talked about this. You're doing me a solid, so I'm footing the bill. This was all already discussed and decided."

"Yeah, but, you're helping me out too ... with Drake."

He released my hand and sat back in the plastic chair, letting out a frustrated sigh.

"Are you in this like you agreed, or are you backing out?"

"I'm in it."

"Great, then how about we agree not to hash this shit out every time I buy you something. The amount of money I spent today was nothing to me, a drop in the bucket. And, while I get not everyone has unlimited funds, and it may make you uncomfortable sometimes, or be a pride issue, it's what we already agreed on. So, don't sweat it. This deal is mutually beneficial. We're in it together, so let's not sweat every little detail, okay?"

I took a deep breath and nodded, because although spending that amount of money was panic-inducing for me, it obviously wasn't to him. I could get over the money, the fancy car, the rich boy attitude, but the mere mention of either of us backing out made my palms sweat and my heart race.

I was already getting used to Ridge, and it seemed I didn't want to lose him. Which, given the nature of our deal, was a bit worrisome.

"Cool. It's settled. Now, what's your schedule look like for the rest of the week? We're having a party at Delta Friday night. It'll be the perfect time to come out as an official couple and validate the rumors that Drake and Caitlyn will have spread."

"Um, I have a scrimmage on Friday evening, but could come after."

"Scrimmage?"

"Yeah, for softball. It's off season, but we still get together a few times a week to work out and work on fundamentals. This is our first scrimmage of the year."

"You play softball? I didn't know…"

I ducked my head and said, "Yup, I'm on a scholarship. I've played my whole life. My dad had a glove on my hand as soon as I could throw a ball."

"That's nice," Ridge said, his tone almost sad. "My father was never the *toss a ball in the backyard* kind of dad."

"That sucks," I murmured, feeling bad that Ridge had missed out on the stuff I'd always taken for granted. "Gosh, I really miss them."

"Who? Your parents?"

I nodded.

"My mom makes the best ribeyes and Judd always makes a big breakfast on Sundays. I even miss Carter's moodiness."

There was a pang in my heart as I thought about how much of Carter's life I'd already missed. How much my family had all changed and grown over the years, just as I had. It was depressing to think we were growing apart.

"That's not something I can even understand," Ridge said, absently reaching for one of my fries and popping it in his mouth.

"Missing your parents?"

He nodded.

"I couldn't get out of there fast enough, and I don't go home unless I absolutely have to. Once Brody is here next year, there'll be even less reason for me to."

"I'm sorry," I said, my heart hurting for him. I couldn't imagine not being close to my family. They were the most important thing in my life.

Ridge shrugged.

"Don't be. Things are better now than they were when I was younger. I no longer have to rely on them for anything, and we're all happier for it."

I was about to ask more about their relationship when he changed the subject.

"So, Friday ... I'll come to your scrimmage and we can go to the party together."

"You can pick me up after the scrimmage, but I don't want you to come."

"Why not? It's our official coming out day, so we may as well let your team in on it as well."

I shook my head.

"I don't like being the center of attention, or having people I know come to my practices or scrimmages. It throws me off my game."

Ridge narrowed his eyes and asked, "Then how do you play in games, if you don't like being watched?"

"Playing a game is different. I'm in the zone and focused on one thing only ... winning. But, in a practice or a scrimmage, we're working on fundamentals, training, and perfecting our ability to work together as a team."

"Do you not let anyone go, or is this just about me? Cause, I promise, I'm not going to be judging you or anything..."

"No, it's not just you, it's anyone. Drake plays baseball, and I wouldn't let him come watch me either ... It's always been a thing with me. Judd was the coach, so he had to be there, but I wouldn't even let my mom watch me at practice, only during games. It's like, my superstition, I guess."

I noticed Ridge's mouth had thinned when I mentioned Drake, which was the second time today he'd had that reaction, but I didn't call him on it. If he was jealous of Drake and me, it was better I didn't know about it, especially after my gut reaction to hearing Caitlyn flirt with him.

Bringing those feelings to light would be treading in dangerous territory.

"Okay, if that's your deal, so be it. Can I pick you up at the field, or do you want me to swing by your apartment after?"

"Come by the field and I'll introduce you to the team," I said, giving him an encouraging smile and hoping my weird softball superstition wasn't a turn off. I didn't want him to think I didn't want him in that part of my life, or that I was embarrassed about him and our relationship.

I mean, our fake relationship.

The tension eased out of him and he grinned back.

"What time?"

"Seven o'clock?"

"I'll be there."

FIFTEEN
RIDGE

The week went by quickly.

All of my professors decided to pile on the homework, we had a board meeting for the frat, and I had some Sergeant at Arms shit to take care of. Basically, keep order during the meeting and make sure everyone was following the rules.

One of our pledges had gotten caught stealing from one of the rooms, so I'd given him a shakedown, with a threat to involve the cops, and when he'd fessed up and returned the goods, I'd shown him the door and told him never to return.

Never a dull moment in the Delta house.

Because we'd both been so busy, I'd shared a few texts with Karrie, but that was all, so I was looking forward to spending some time with her at the party.

The strumming in my veins as I walked across the field felt a lot like anticipation, but I didn't question it. Karrie and I were friends, right? Partners. So, it was a good thing that I enjoyed spending time with her.

It didn't mean anything other than that...

At least, that's the shit I tried to feed myself as I caught sight of her standing with some girls from her team and had to force myself to continue to walk slowly, rather than jog toward her like an asshole.

One of the girls looked up as I approached and said something to the group, which had them all turning my way.

When Karrie's gaze landed on me, her face lit up, and I swear she looked just like I felt.

She broke away, and when *she* started jogging toward *me*, my heart jumped and my face split with a grin. I could tell she was going to launch herself at me, so I stopped and braced, then opened my arms to catch her.

Karrie jumped into them and fused her lips to mine.

Just as I was about to deepen the kiss, my fingers flexing on her ass, she pulled back and smiled down at me.

"Are they watching?" she whispered.

I looked over her shoulder and nodded.

"Good. They didn't believe me when I said I was dating you, so I had to make it convincing."

Disappointment crashed through me as I lowered her to the ground.

Of course her greeting had all been for show ... Stupid of me to forget my own game.

"Why wouldn't they believe you?" I asked, schooling my features so as not to give away too much.

She wrinkled her nose and said, "They don't think you're my type, and they definitely don't think I'm yours."

I took a moment to look her over and thought the baseball cap she was wearing made her look ridiculously adorable. And, I wasn't mad about the tight pants either.

"That should shut them up then," I replied, taking her hand in mine and walking her toward the girls, who were all watching us like hawks. "And, if they still have doubts, we'll dispel them now."

Karrie nodded and called, "Hey, guys, this is Ridge, for those of you who don't know him."

Multiple hot glances were sent my way, along with a few judgy looks, and one outright scowl.

I figured the latter two were the girls on the team who were actually Karrie's friends, the former obviously were more interested in their own social standing and getting an itch scratched than in having her best interest at heart.

I ignored the thirsty girls and smiled at the rest.

"Ladies," I said, my voice deep.

There were a few titters and fluttering eyelashes as Karrie placed her hand on my abs and smiled up at me.

"Ridge, this is my team..." she said, naming off a bunch of names I didn't bother to remember.

"It was nice to meet you," I said graciously, then decided to embolden them even more by offering, "And, if you're free tonight, we're having a party at Delta. It's always the hottest spot on Friday night. Just tell the guy at the door that I invited you."

Karrie's fingers flexed on my abs and I knew she was pleased with the invite.

We said our goodbyes and, after Karrie grabbed her gear, we started to the parking lot.

"Do we need to load up your bike?" I asked as our feet hit asphalt.

She shook her head.

"I walked. It's not that far, and it's a good way to warm up my legs before I get here and the real workout begins."

I opened the car door for her, before rounding my baby and getting in the driver's side.

She was right, the fields weren't far from her apartment; still, I felt a strange niggle of worry at the thought of her walking to and from the fields alone, especially now that it was starting to get dark earlier.

"I can drive you home whenever you have practice, if you want," I said. When I noticed her head swing toward me, I added, "You know, to keep up appearances and cement our relationship for your team."

Karrie let out a little laugh.

"You know, some of the girls went absolutely nutso when I mentioned your name earlier. I guess since I didn't know who you were when we met, I didn't realize what a hot commodity you are on campus. I mean, damn, Ridge, Tish and Julie were practically green with envy."

"This is what I've been trying to tell you this whole time," I said, going for my usual cockiness, even though I wasn't quite feeling it. "I'm kind of a big deal."

SIXTEEN
KARRIE

"You dating Ridge is seriously the best thing that's ever happened to me," Mina said happily as she danced in the center of the crowd at Delta house.

A bubble of laughter left my throat.

"That's happened to *you?*"

She nodded emphatically.

"Free booze, hot guys, and unfettered access to Delta parties? This is every co-ed's wet dream," she said loudly over the music.

I smiled, indicating I'd heard her, but kept dancing rather than shouting back. This wasn't the best place to have a conversation, and since we'd only been dancing for two songs, I wasn't ready to stop.

I'd had a Captain and Coke when we'd arrived, just to take the edge off of my fear. But, I needn't have been afraid. It wasn't like Ridge had made a big announcement, or even introduced me around like I had with him to the team.

We'd walked in together, he'd kissed me a couple times, and when any guys had tried to come up and talk to me, he'd glared at them.

And, that, my friends, was Ridge's way of telling everyone that we're together. Kind of the frat boy equivalent of peeing around me and marking his territory.

I didn't mind, especially since Mina was with me. It wasn't like I wanted to have conversations with these guys and have to lie to their faces. It was easier to let them make assumptions based off of Ridge's actions.

I'd also seen the benefit, when Drake had taken one look at Ridge's arm around my shoulder and his face pinched so hard he looked constipated.

I moved with the music, feeling confident and sexy in the new tube dress Ridge bought for me the other day. Mina'd been so excited when I'd actually done my hair and makeup *and* put on a dress for this party.

She thought Ridge had helped me finally get out of the funk I'd been in since Drake, and I guess he had. Because, even though it all started out as a hoax, I was really starting to like Ridge.

Heck, when I'd seen him at the fields earlier, my stupid heart had been so happy it flipped in my chest.

As I danced, I surveyed the room, my gaze flitting over hundreds of scantily clad, sweaty bodies and more Polo shirts than should be allowed in one space, until it landed on Ridge. He was sitting on a sofa, which had been pushed up against the wall, laughing with Wes and some guy I'd never met.

Feeling my eyes on him, Ridge's head lifted, and when he found me looking he lifted his chin in acknowledgement and gave me a cocky grin.

This time, other parts of my body took notice, as I studied his ridiculously handsome face and enjoyed the way his biceps seemed to be fighting against the constraint of his gray V-neck. I found myself wondering what the bit of stubble on his face would feel like against my skin.

Whoa, where'd that come from?

I blinked and quickly turned my attention back to Mina, who'd stopped dancing and was fanning herself.

"Air," she yelled.

I nodded and was about to go with her outside, when a cute guy with dark skin and a close-shaved beard walked straight up to her and said something in her ear. When she looked him up and down and gave him a coy smile, then looked at me and winked, I figured she'd rather I didn't.

As they walked away, Mina looked over her shoulder at me and mouthed, *Wow*.

I gave her a thumb's up, before turning and seeing that Ridge was still on the couch. Wanting to play my part in our little charade, I sauntered over to him and eased myself onto his lap.

Ridge didn't even blink, he simply put his arm around me and pulled me back so I was fit snug against him.

"Hey, Karrie," Wes said in greeting.

"Hey," I replied as I tried to tug the bottom of my dress down so I wouldn't inadvertently flash Ridge's brother. "How's rush going so far?"

"Good, but, I gotta say, between rush, swim practice, and classes, I'm spread pretty thin. I wouldn't even be at this party if it wasn't mandatory for pledges to attend," he said, looking around the room. "In fact, I've probably been sitting too long. I don't want the other guys to think I'm getting special treatment because my brother's the Sergeant at Arms."

Wes stood up and said, "Good to see you again."

"Same," I replied with a smile, shifting to move off of Ridge's lap and take the spot he'd vacated, when Ridge's arm tightened, holding me in place.

I looked at him curiously.

"Stay," he said softly, the rough timber of his voice causing goosebumps to break out across my arms.

His hand moved lower until his fingertips were grazing the skin on my thigh just below the hem of my dress, caressing me softly, slowly.

My breath caught in my throat as I watched the blue in his eyes darken.

I shifted slightly, suddenly hyperaware of every place our bodies were in contact. His chest, my back, our thighs, my ass and his...

"*Karrie.*"

It took a moment, but eventually I realized the sound of my name being called was coming from behind me, so I pulled my eyes from the tractor beam of Ridge's gaze to see Drake standing there.

His sudden presence was like a bucket of ice water had been thrown on my head.

"What?" I asked, looking around, expecting his new girlfriend to be latched on to his arm like always, but, surprisingly, he was alone.

"Can I talk to you?"

"Why?"

Drake looked from me to Ridge and scowled.

"Come on, Karrie, just for a minute."

"Fine," I said, pushing up off of Ridge and standing in front of Drake. "Talk."

"Come outside. It's too loud in here."

I looked down at Ridge, whose hard expression was focused on my ex, and said, "I'll be right back."

"Here if you need me," he replied, and I liked his response so much, I leaned down to give him a quick kiss on the lips in thanks. Because that's what I'd do if he actually was my boyfriend.

When I straightened back up I looked at Drake and said, "After you," holding my hand out toward the back door.

I followed him outside, made a mental note that Mina was currently sitting on the porch swing making out with the hot guy she'd left the dance floor with, and crossed my arms as I turned my attention back to Drake.

"Talk," I said again, really not wanting to hear anything he had to say. In fact, I found myself mentally cursing him for interrupting whatever it was that had been happening back there between me and Ridge.

"What are you doing with that asshole?" he shot out, causing me to turn on my heel and start marching back inside.

Drake put his hand on my arm to stop me, and although I did, I glanced down at it before looking pointedly back at him.

He dropped his hand.

"I'm serious, Karebear, he's no good for you."

"First of all, never call me that again, you lost that right when you dumped me. Second, it's none of your goddamn business who I choose to spend my time with. You moved on way before I did, so I really don't understand why it matters to you anyway."

"Because he's a total dick," Drake yelled in frustration.

"Yeah, well, so are you," I returned. "Now, I'm going back in there to be with my boyfriend, and I'd appreciate it if you left us alone. *Forever*."

"Boyfriend? *Karrie*," he called, but I'd already turned to find Mina and her guy standing behind me.

Mina moved so I could pass and go inside, and as I walked away I heard her say, "You heard her, Drake. Get lost and stay gone."

SEVENTEEN
RIDGE

I clenched my fist, eyes on the door Karrie walked out with Drake.

I hated that she was out there with him, but knew things were falling into place. The plan was to get Drake jealous, and it was obviously working. Dude's eyes had nearly bugged out of his head when he got a load of Karrie in that dress.

I'd wanted to break his nose.

I downed my beer and vaguely listened to Javi, our recruitment chair, talk about the threesome he'd had the night before.

Dude was connoisseur of women.

The tension in my shoulders eased as Karrie came storming back into the room, Mina and Trap, one of my brothers, trailing behind her. I kept my eyes on the door, but Drake didn't follow.

Thank fuck.

I stood as she approached, because although feeling her supple ass on my cock had been amazing, I knew it wasn't in the best interest of our pact to play with fire like that. Before Drake had come up, I'd been seconds away from pushing the boundaries of our relationship.

"How'd that go?" I asked her when she stopped in front of me.

"Fine. He wanted to warn me off you. I basically told him to go fuck himself," she seethed.

With her cheeks flushed, chest heaving, and eyes blazing, she looked hot as fuck. Add all that to the fact she was wearing a dress made to make a man beg for mercy, and Karrie was one dangerous package.

"That's rich, coming from him," I managed, lifting my chin at Trap in greeting.

Not wanting the others to hear, while still playing the game, I leaned in close and brushed my lips against her neck and whispered, "We have him right where we want him."

Karrie clutched my shoulders in a way that let me know she was just as affected by me as I was by her.

"You think so?" she breathed.

I nodded and sucked her skin lightly, before pulling back.

"One hundred percent."

I wanted to say more, to assure her that Drake would be begging her to come back before the holidays, but Mina and Trap were still next to us, and I didn't want her best friend to become suspicious of our relationship.

Plus, the thought of Drake making a move on Karrie filled me with a rage that was confusing, and I found myself hating the fact that she was so focused on getting her revenge. I'd be happier if she left Drake firmly in the rearview, where he belonged.

"What's up, *bros and hoes?*"

Knowing it was Crush before turning, I already wore a scowl before replying, "Crush, don't call women *hoes*."

"Sorry, *Rigid*," he replied with a smirk.

What a fuckin' ass.

"Whoa, who's this hottie?" Crush continued, his eyes all over Karrie in a way that made me long to kick him in the balls.

"Karrie," my date replied drolly. "We met last week at the rush event."

"No shit?" he asked giving her another onceover. "Damn, Ridge, you are obviously *winning*. Her makeover is next level."

"We aren't in the competition, I already told you that. Karrie and I were only participating to help Delta. And, I'd appreciate it if you'd stop fuckin' ogling my girlfriend, man," I told him, my tone ensuring him I was *not* bullshitting.

Crush's eyes widened as he swung to face me.

"Girlfriend?"

I expected my brothers to be surprised. Most of us enjoyed the life being a single Delta provided, and I'd been no different over the last three years.

"That's right," I said, putting an arm around Karrie's waist and pulling her in tight.

His slow blink was comical, but when he looked back at Karrie he muttered, "I can see that," then he shook his head as if to clear it, before tilting back his neck and shouting, "*Deltas ... drink!*"

It was kind of our party battle cry, so all the Deltas responded by answering, "*Drink*," and chugging whatever they were drinking.

Once Crush finished his beer, he glanced at me once more and said, "Congrats," before wandering off to bother someone else.

"*Ugh, that guy*," Karrie muttered, her voice laced with disgust.

"Yeah, ugh," Mina agreed, before looking at me and saying, "That was hot though. The way you jumped to our defense and claimed Karrie. He's a keeper," she told Karrie, who looked up at me thoughtfully.

"Yeah, I think you're right," she murmured, her eyes softening and lips turning up slowly.

Jesus.

I'd thought it was bad when she was sitting on my lap. But, her looking at me the way she was right then, made me want to throw her over my shoulder, take her to my room, and spend the rest of the night inside of her.

The need for space felt suddenly suffocating.

I looked at my phone, pretended to see something important, and swore under my breath.

"You know what?" I began, shaking my head and frowning. "I totally forgot I have a paper due Monday and I haven't even started it yet. I think I'm gonna call it early so I can get to it first thing tomorrow."

I saw the surprise on Karrie's face before it was replaced with understanding.

"Oh, okay, I'm actually tired myself. I'm not used to going out as much as I have since I met you," she explained with a small smile. "Plus, scrimmages always take it out of me. I'll just head home and we can both get some rest."

God, I am such a dick.

"I'll give you a ride home," I offered, hoping to soften my abrupt decision.

"Actually, Trap and I were about to head to the apartment. Karrie can ride with us, right, Trap?" Mina asked.

"Yup."

"Great, so it's settled. Focus on your paper and we'll talk Monday, okay?" Karrie asked sweetly.

She was being so understanding I felt even more like a douche.

"Yeah, and if I get done earlier, I'll call you," I lied.

There was no paper, and I really needed the weekend to put some distance between us before I did something I'd regret. We only had one more week until the Homecoming party, and another couple until Thanksgiving.

Keeping things platonic was the best course of action.

"Sounds good," Karrie said, then got closer to me and tilted her head back slightly.

Knowing what she wanted, and cognizant of the audience present, I complied and lowered my face to meet hers.

The kiss was brief, but soft and achingly sweet.

When she stepped back, she said, "Get some rest and focus."

"Goodnight, killer," I replied softly.

She gave me a little wave and followed her friend through the crowd.

Not wanting to be any more of a liar than I already was, and no longer feeling the atmosphere, I strode through the crush of people and up the stairs to my room. Once there, I grabbed a bottle of whiskey out of my cabinet and sat on the bed.

I was going to get wasted and come up with a plan to keep my pact with Karrie without doing something stupid.

Like falling for her.

EIGHTEEN
KARRIE

"I'm so glad we're doing this," I told Mina as I carried my slice of meatlovers pizza and glass of our cheap box of cabernet wine to the couch.

"Me, too. It's nice to take a Saturday night off once in a while."

She was speaking for herself, of course. Although I'd spent plenty weekends at home since *the humiliating dump*, Mina was a veritable party animal. When I'd suggested we stay home and have a girl's night, I figured she'd already have plans, but she'd happily agreed.

"Yes, especially with such great company," I replied with a smile.

I felt my face mask crack at the movement and glanced at my roommate's matching charcoal mask.

"I think these are ready to come off," I told her.

"Yeah, let's wash them off before we start the show back up."

We were currently on our third series binge of *Sex and the City*. It was our favorite go-to show.

We washed our faces until they were shiny and clean,

rearranged our messy buns, and went back to the living room to resume eating, drinking, and crushing on Mr. Big.

I was two glasses of wine in when it occurred to me that I should probably text Ridge and check up on him. He'd acted a little strange at the party; at least, as far as I knew, it was strange. In truth I'd only known him a few weeks, so he could always be moody and I just hadn't learned it about him yet.

Whatever the case, I was taking him at his word and believing that he was busy with homework this weekend, and that's why he hadn't asked me to sleep over again, and hadn't called or texted me since we'd left Delta house.

We'd had a pretty hot moment before Drake had interrupted us, so it was possible he was putting on the brakes a little because of it.

Maybe he was as ill-prepared for our chemistry as I was...

Or, maybe those feelings were all on my end, he thought of me as an annoying little sister, and he was home writing his paper, while I was in my apartment having inappropriate thoughts of how it would feel to have his hands all over my body.

Making progress?

I figured a text that was simple and to the point, while still letting him know that I was his partner, was the way to go.

Because what I really wanted to text was, **Could your cock possibly be as big as it felt on my ass?**

Luckily, I wasn't that drunk ... *yet*.

"Hey ... no phones," Mina complained when she caught me looking down instead of at the TV.

"Sorry, I was just checking on Ridge."

"Have you talked to him today?" she asked.

I shook my head.

"Okay, fine, then you can text, but only to make sure he

hasn't been so wrapped up in work that he's forgotten to eat or shower."

Yeah, it's going good here. You good?

Yup. Chilling at home with Mina.

Cool. Anymore chatter from your useless ex?

Nope, all quiet.

Good. Lunch tomorrow?

Sounds good. Just text me where and when.

Will do.

Goodnight!

Night.

"So?" Mina asked when I put down the phone.

"He's good. We're meeting for lunch tomorrow," I replied, relieved and feeling silly for worrying so much when things were obviously fine.

"Nice. Maybe lunch and a nooner," she said, making me laugh when she wiggled her eyebrows at me.

"What? No ... we aren't having sex," I told her, tucking my legs underneath me.

"You mean, like, you're not having sex tomorrow, or at all?"

"I mean we haven't had sex *yet*."

"Really?" Mina asked, her expression clearly asking, *why not?*

"Yes, *really*. Ridge is the first guy I've dated since Drake. I want to take things slow and make sure it's right before I jump into bed with him. I don't want to get hurt again," I told her, which was a true statement, even if the likelihood of Ridge and I ever having sex was basically zero.

"Slow is for suckers and high school kids. That man is deliciously tall, cut, and those eyes could make a woman spontaneously combust. Honestly, I don't know how you've been able to control yourself. I would've ridden him like a Harley ... full throttle."

"You have issues," I told her, unable to control my laughter when she stood up and pretended she was riding a vibrating motorcycle around the living room.

"You love it," she shot back.

"I really do. The day I met you was the luckiest day of my life."

"Hey," Mina said, putting down the kickstand on the bike so she could join me on the couch and pull me in for a hug. "I love you, Karebear."

"Love you, too, Ermina."

NINETEEN
RIDGE

"Hey, brother, how's things?" I asked Brody.

I'd been in my room, lying back on my bed and pondering my life choices, specifically my relationship with Karrie and what I was going to do about it, when I'd remembered what Wes had told me.

I still hadn't reached out to our little brother. So, I'd picked up my cell and called him.

"Can't complain," Brody replied, sounding tired.

"Did I wake you?"

He yawned. "Mmhmm, I was out late last night."

"Yeah, I've heard complaints about your active social life," I told him, annoyed on his behalf.

"From who, Mom?"

"Hell no, you know I only talk to her by force ... It was passed along by her favorite child."

Brody snorted.

"I don't know how he still buys her shit."

"Me neither, man. I guess he feels sorry for her," I replied. "You know Wes is the bleeding heart of the group."

"This is true."

"So, seriously, how's everything going? School good? Your grades holding up? You know you can't slack off senior year, no matter how tempting it may be." I know I sounded like his dad, rather than his brother, but I also knew our parents weren't staying on top of his education.

"I know ... don't worry. I want to get the hell out of here, so there's no way I'd mess up my chance to join you guys at U of M."

"Good," I said, and when I heard a knock on my door, I moved the phone away from my mouth and yelled, "Come in!"

The door opened and Wes peeked around the corner.

"Speak of the devil," I muttered, waving my other brother inside.

Wes shut the door behind him and mouthed, *"Brody?"*

I nodded.

"Is it Wes?" Brody asked.

"Yep."

"Tell him I say, hey, and to stop talkin' shit."

I repeated his words to Wes, who shook his head and stuck up his middle finger.

"He said, *fuck off*," I told Brody.

Brody chuckled and asked, "We done here? I'm going back to sleep."

"Yeah, we're done. Just keep your grades up and your nose clean. We'll see you at Thanksgiving."

"See ya," he said, and hung up.

I threw my phone on the bed next to me and asked Wes, "What's up?"

He crossed to sit in my chair.

"Not much, I was downstairs doing KP duty and thought I'd stop up and see how you're doing before I go meet Trixie."

"How's that going?" I asked, searching my memory banks for an image of his makeover girl.

He shrugged.

"Initially it seemed like she wasn't really interested in the whole rush thing, but she's been asking me so many questions about the process and the Deltas that I feel like maybe her reluctance was all for show."

"You been working on the makeover yet?"

"Yeah, we have to check in with Crush every few days and give him an update on our progress. We've already been to the salon for hair, makeup, and nails, and we've gone shopping a couple times."

Wes sounded as if the process had been as much fun as a root canal, which to him it probably had been.

"How about you? How are things with Karrie? I gotta say, you shocked the hell out of me when you introduced her. Is it serious?" he asked, and I knew this was the in I needed.

I looked at my brother and realized not only was this the perfect opportunity to move forward with my plan, but maybe I could also get some advice on my relationship with Karrie. The actual relationship, not the fake one.

I hadn't lied when I said my brother had no game when it came to women, but that wasn't the kind of information I needed. No, not only was he the sensitive brother, but he was the only one who'd had a serious girlfriend, and one of the only people in the world I felt comfortable talking about myself with.

This was perfect.

"Actually, I'd like to talk to you about that," I began.

"You would?" he asked, looking pleased and sitting up a little taller.

"Yeah, man, I'm in unchartered waters here..."

"So, it *is* serious."

I nodded.

"Yeah, I think it is. I mean, she's great ... funny, smart, athletic, and she doesn't take any shit. She doesn't care about our money, who our family is, or any of that. Karrie's the real deal. And the chemistry? We haven't actually done anything other than kiss, but anytime our skin comes in contact, it's like ... boom."

"You haven't done anything more than kiss? You? My brother, *Ridge?*"

"Fuck off," I replied, causing him to throw up his hands and laugh.

"I'm just sayin', it's pretty out of character," Wes said with a chuckle.

"I know, that's why I need help. This girl's got me totally off balance. She's everything I've said I didn't want, especially while I'm still in school, but now that she's in my life, I don't want to let her go."

"Then ... don't."

"But what about my rules? My plans? I've always been more of a casual relationship kind of guy, and nothing about what I feel for Karrie is casual. In fact, I'm thinking of taking her home for Thanksgiving."

Wes's eyes widened. "No shit?"

"No shit."

"You should go for it."

"But, what if I'm no good for her?" I ask, admitting my worst fear. "What if I'm like Dad?"

Wes scowled and stood up.

"Ridge, you're nothing like that asshole. You're always upfront with everyone and you've never cheated. You don't use your fists to solve things, or to prove you're in charge ... And, even though you and Mom don't get along, you've always been there for Brody and I. You were our protector, and more of a father to us than Dad ever was. Karrie would be lucky to have you."

Shit. I blinked back the emotion that suddenly felt like hot needles in my throat. It felt good to know he thought that about me.

When my feelings were locked down, I stood up and moved to pull him in for a quick, one-armed hug.

"Thanks, Wes."

"Yeah of course. Thanks for talking to me about it ... I think Karrie's great. She's the yin to your yang. Bring her home, Brody will love her."

He didn't mention Mom's reaction, and neither did I, because we both knew how Susan Temple was going to feel about Karrie and I being a couple ... *She'd fuckin' hate it.*

Which was the whole point.

TWENTY
KARRIE

I fought back the urge to run to the diner, instead forcing myself to take my time and walk like a normal person, even though I was really excited to see Ridge again.

It had only been three days, but I'd missed him.

I may have been able to control my feet, but there was no stopping the smile that spread across my face when I saw him sitting in a booth in the back when I walked inside.

He looked so handsome.

His hair was long on top, but perfectly styled, and the stubble on his face had filled in more, making him look older and even more delectable. I don't know how it was possible for him to look even hotter than usual, but somehow he did.

Or, maybe I was just looking at him with new eyes.

Lustful eyes.

Ridge's head came up and his mouth turned up when he saw me, which made my stomach dip and my heart do a funny flip.

"Hi," I said, even though I was farther away than I'd initially thought and spoke a little too loudly.

"Hey, babe," he replied, causing a thrill to rip through me at the nickname.

That's new, I thought. But found I really, *really* liked it.

I scooted into the seat across from him and tossed my crossbody shoulder bag down next to me.

To my surprise, Ridge got up, leaned over the table, and gave me a lingering kiss. I figured it was because we were in a local place, which was a hot spot for other students, but I enjoyed it nonetheless.

Ridge took his seat just as the server came to the table.

"What can I get for you?" the friendly older woman with a nametag that said, *Hazel*, asked.

"I'll have the cheeseburger combo with a Coke," I replied.

"Same," Ridge added, his smile devastating enough to make the poor woman do a double-take before leaving to put in our order.

"So, how'd your paper go?" I asked him once we were alone.

"Good."

When he didn't expand further, I asked, "Did you do anything else over the weekend? Anything fun?"

"Not really. Just hung around the house. I did have a good conversation with Wes, and checked in with Brody. What about you?"

"Hung out with Mina and got some homework done. That's about it."

"What do you have going on this week, anything?" he asked.

I thanked Hazel for our Cokes before replying.

"Nothing big. I'm going to meet some of my teammates at the gym on Tuesday and Thursday. I have a quiz, I think ... and then Homecoming."

"You planning on going to the game?"

I shrugged.

"I guess I hadn't really thought about it."

"Well, you can come with me, if you want. Most of the Deltas will be there since we have a couple guys on the team. The pledges will be back getting the house ready for the party that night."

"Sounds good to me."

Honestly, Ridge could ask me to go with him to watch a table tennis tournament, and I'd probably say yes. That's how much I enjoyed being around him.

"Great," he said, his blue eyes shining. "And, I was thinking if you're not busy, we could go see the new Marvel movie on Wednesday night."

"Oh, I've been wanting to see that. Where, the multiplex?"

Ridge's lip curled up and I bit back a laugh.

"Seriously? *No*," he exclaimed. "I went to that place once my freshman year and vowed to never return. The seats are uncomfortable, the popcorn is stale, and the sound system sucked. We'll go to the place downtown with the bar and reclining seats."

"Wow, so not even the local theater is good enough for you? You have to go to the fancy-pants place twenty minutes away?" I joked.

"Have you ever been there?"

"No, Ridge," I said with mock patience. "I'm a college student on scholarship. I don't throw my money away on reclining seats when there's a perfectly good theater a mile from my house."

"I promise, once you go there, you'll be ruined for anything else."

"Maybe I shouldn't go then."

Ridge scoffed.

"*We're going*. Not only is it comfortable with surround sound, but they deliver the food and drinks right to your seat. You're going to love it."

"Okay, but I hope I'm not devastated when I'm delegated back to food courts and multiplexes."

"Nah, you're with me now ... It's only the best from now on," Ridge replied cockily, and although I smiled, I couldn't help but wonder if he meant it.

After all, the pact only lasted until we got back from Thanksgiving break.

I couldn't expect him to foot the bill indefinitely. Once the pact was over, I'd feel guilty having him pay my way, and I couldn't afford to live the way he did. *Not many people could.* Would he still want to be friends and hang out, or would I be dropped for the friends who were in his social class?

"Ridge, you can't pay for me forever," I said, deciding to lay it out.

He reached across the table and laid his hand over mine. "Of course I can, you're my girl."

I furrowed my brow and looked around us to see if anyone was listening. They weren't.

"Only for a couple more weeks," I whispered.

"Let's just play it by ear," Ridge said with a wink, letting my hand go when Hazel arrived with our food.

What the heck did he mean by that?

TWENTY-ONE
RIDGE

The more I thought about things ... me and Karrie, my conversation with my brother, my parents and family relationships, the more I wondered if I was being too cautious. And, if I was letting fear hold me back.

I'd always thought of myself as a casual kind of guy, interested in hookups and sex, but not anything deeper.

But, now that I'd met and spent time with Karrie, I was starting to think the baggage from my childhood was possibly standing in the way of something amazing. I'd always been so adamant about not getting too serious, that if I didn't get my head out of my ass, I could let the most amazing girl I'd ever met slip through my fingers.

I was cockblocking myself.

Before we'd met for lunch, I'd decided I was going to get out of my own way and see what happened.

Let nature take its course, if you will.

I'd started by letting myself be affectionate with Karrie when the mood struck, rather than keeping myself tethered, and by asking her out on a date. She'd seemed a little surprised at first, but not at all turned off.

In fact, if I wasn't mistaken, she'd been looking at me with the same desire and curiosity I felt for her.

I'd been anticipating our night out ever since, and when I picked her up for the movies, I wasn't disappointed. Wearing skintight jeans, a green tank, and a million-dollar smile, Karrie'd returned my hug of greeting with gusto.

As we drove to the theater, I took her hand in mine and listened while she chatted about what she'd been up to.

"I took the coward's way out and texted my mom about Thanksgiving," she was saying, her lilting voice and laughter filling the space around us. "To say she's not pleased would be an understatement."

"Sorry, I didn't even think about the effect your missing a holiday at home would have on your family," I said, kind of surprised that I actually did feel bad.

Being a selfish person by nature, when I'd brought up the stipulation about going home with me for Thanksgiving, the fact that she'd have to cancel her own plans had never even crossed my mind.

See, I am a dick.

"Oh, it's not a big deal," Karrie assured me with a smile. "It's not like I'm missing Christmas or something. She's just disappointed because she was expecting me to come home."

After parking, we went inside and placed our food and drink orders. I'd already purchased our tickets through the app, to ensure we had good seats and weren't stuck up in the first row with a shitty view of the screen.

"Wow, fancy," Karrie laughed as she sat down and reclined her seat.

"Told you it was great," I replied, reclining my own seat before pushing up the arm that separated us.

With that barrier gone, I moved to put my arm around her and pull her closer.

She looked up at me, lips parted with surprise, but didn't protest or move away, so I took that as a good sign.

When the lights dimmed and the previews started, I turned my face toward her and moved my free hand up to cup her cheek. Karrie looked up at me, her expression expectant, and something else...

Hopeful, maybe?

I moved slowly, giving her time to stop me if she wanted, before capturing her lips with mine.

The kiss began soft, sweet ... searching, but when Karrie's tongue darted out and caressed my lower lip, I angled my head and deepened the kiss, showing her what I'd so far been unable to put into words.

How much I wanted her.

She shifted toward me in her seat, one hand coming up to touch my face, while the other fisted in my shirt at my side.

I pulled her tighter and lost myself in her, growing needier and greedier with each little moan that escaped her lips.

We stopped to take a breath, foreheads resting against each other, both softly panting, and then Karrie said my name on a moan before grasping the back of my head and pulling me down as she lifted her lips to mine.

This time, she took the lead, her lips soft and supple, her hand moving from the fabric of my shirt to the skin underneath.

I was ready to pull her on top of me, and urge her to straddle me in the seat, not giving a fuck where the hell we were, when I heard a throat clearing loudly beside us and felt a tap on my shoulder.

I pulled away and glared at the pimply faced teenager who was looking at me with a red face.

"What?" I barked, tucking Karrie's head into my neck so he couldn't look at her.

"Uh, sorry, sir, but we have your food, and, uh, the movie's about to start. You can't, uh, go at it like that in here," he managed, his voice shaking so bad it would have been funny if I didn't currently want to break his face for interrupting us.

Karrie released me and moved over into her seat.

We both put down our trays so the kid could deliver our food before scurrying away.

Once he was gone I looked at Karrie and asked, "You okay?"

She flushed and nodded.

I leaned over and whispered, "Sorry, I guess I got carried away."

Her eyes were big when she looked at me, but she was smiling when she replied, "That's okay, I did, too."

I grinned at her, happy that she didn't seem to regret our little makeout session, and lifted her hand to kiss the back of her knuckles, before settling back to enjoy the movie.

TWENTY-TWO
KARRIE

I'd been floating on a cloud for the last few days.

Any time Ridge and I weren't in class or I wasn't training, we'd spent together. Talking, laughing, and kissing. Lots and lots of kissing.

It was fun, easy, and utterly frustrating.

Neither of us had brought up the change in our relationship. There no longer had to be people around for us to show affection; in fact, we were usually alone. But Ridge never took it further than kissing, and when I tried, he backed off.

The funny thing was, since the day we'd met we'd always talked things out. The pact, our expectations, and everything in between. But neither of us had used our voices when it came to what we were doing now.

Maybe we were scared, or worried that talking about it would scare the other person off.

Or, maybe we were just unsure of what in the hell it was we were doing, and wanted to explore a little more before labeling it.

All I knew, on my end, was we needed to progress from kissing because I was walking around with the female equivalent to blue balls. I'm talking a constant state of *horny*. I didn't know how Ridge did it...

But, I was hoping tonight was the night.

Mina was at Trap's place and Ridge was coming over for dinner, which I was making for us, and we were going to watch some Netflix.

And, yes, I am totally hoping Netflix was code for having lots and lots of sex.

I'd just finished mixing the salad and pulling garlic bread out of the oven when I heard a knock at the door. My heart leapt and my tummy dropped as I hurried to the door, then stopped to compose myself so I wouldn't look like I was too eager, and opened the door.

My jaw dropped when standing on the other side was not Ridge, but my parents.

"Mom?" I asked, confused and taken aback. "What are you guys doing here?"

My mom pulled me in for a quick hug and kiss before pushing past me and walking into the apartment.

"You sent that crazy text about not coming for Thanksgiving and I haven't heard from you since. I had to come and make sure you weren't being held against your will."

I blinked up at Judd.

"Hi, Dad," I said as he bent to kiss my cheek.

"Sorry, Karebear, she was on a rampage. I couldn't stop her from coming to make sure you weren't tied to a chair."

I looked out into the empty hall for a second, then closed the door and turned to lean back against it.

"Mom, I'm okay. I'm sorry if you were worried, *but*, you could have just called, you didn't have to drive all the way out here."

"I had to see for myself that you were okay," my mom said. She held her stomach and asked, "Is that spaghetti?"

I followed her into the kitchen, with Judd trailing behind us.

"She wouldn't let us stop to eat," my dad complained.

"We needed to get here quickly, so we only stopped when absolutely necessary," she explained.

"Apparently, eating is no longer a necessity," he countered dryly, but his expression was full of love as he grinned at my mom.

"*Oh, stop,*" she laughed, lifting the lid off the pot and sniffing. "Wow, you made a lot. Are you meal prepping?"

I shifted from one foot to the other and her eyes narrowed.

"Judd, honey, would you be a sweetheart and bring up our bags?"

"Will do," he replied, turning to leave and shooting me a wink.

"Bags? Plural?" I asked. "How long are you staying?"

"Well, we figured we'd go with you to the Homecoming game this weekend and head home from there. Is that okay?" she asked, still watching me closely. For what, I wasn't sure, but the woman was like a human lie detector test, so I had to tread carefully.

"Of course, you guys can stay as long as you want ... you know that," I replied, but I looked over my shoulder at the door and frowned.

"Are you waiting for someone? Ermina?"

"Oh, no, actually, Mina's ... out. Um, I'm not sure when she'll be home." I wasn't going to tell my mom that Mina was at Trap's getting lucky, which I would obviously never be.

"Then, who's the dinner for?" she persisted.

I sighed and crossed to the island.

Once I was seated across from her, I grabbed a piece of bread and broke it apart before replying, "A guy."

Mom leaned forward on her elbows and asked, "*Oh, really?*"

I chuckled. "Yes, really. It's pretty new, but I like him a lot."

"Is he better than *that Drake*?"

Ever since Drake dumped me, my mom referred to him as *that Drake*.

"Well, obviously I think so, or I wouldn't give him the time of day," I replied.

"Tell me about him," she said, picking up a piece of my bread and popping it in her mouth. "Is he nice?"

"He is ... He's nice, funny, and a little cocky. He's the oldest of three brothers, and next year all three of them will be here together. He's the Sergeant at Arms in his fraternity, and he's tidy, sweet, and totally smart."

"Hmmm, *cocky*, huh?" she asked with a frown, picking up on the one descriptor that could be seen as negative.

"Yeah," I laughed, "but in the best possible way. He comes from money, so sometimes he's a little out of touch with reality, at least, *my* kind of reality, but he's not a jerk or anything."

The door opened and my dad came in carrying two duffel bags.

"Look who I found in the hallway," he said, looking pointedly at me as he walked through the living room.

I hurried over to see Ridge standing in the doorway to my apartment looking adorably confused.

Before I could give him a warning, I heard my mom say from right behind me, "So, you must be the reason Karebear's not coming home for Thanksgiving."

Ridge's gaze swung from her to me, and when I saw he was ready to bolt, I mouthed, *run!*

TWENTY-THREE
RIDGE

I didn't run.

Instead, I turned on the charm and sat down to dinner with Karrie and her parents.

Parents loved me, so I wasn't worried about that. No, the worry was that this was too soon. Yes, I realized I'd be taking Karrie home to meet my mom in a few short weeks, but it wasn't at all the same.

I didn't care what my parents thought about me, my life, or who I was dating.

Karrie, on the other hand, loved her family and took their thoughts and opinions into account. Meeting the parents for her would mean something totally different than it did to me. On one hand, I wanted them to like and approve of our relationship. On the other, I didn't *want* to care what they thought, because *I* didn't even know where this thing between Karrie and I was going.

"Can you pass the bread, Ridge?"

I lifted the plate with the remaining pieces of garlic bread and passed them to Sam, Karrie's mother.

"Thanks," she said politely.

I was struck again by how different Karrie looked from her family. Obviously, Judd wasn't her real father, but while Karrie had blonde curls and blue eyes, Sam's eyes were green and her hair auburn.

I gave Sam a smile and a nod, before turning to Judd and asking, "So, sir, Karrie told me you played professional baseball."

"Call me Judd, and yes, I did play a season in the minor leagues. It was an amazing experience. I made friends for life, and my father traveled to see every game I played. It was a dream come true for both of us."

"If you don't mind my asking, why'd you only play one season?"

Judd smiled at Sam and Karrie.

"I missed my girls and knew starting our life together as a family was more important to me than the game. I'm happy I took my shot on the team, but I've never regretted my decision to leave. I've lived a charmed life."

I was surprised to see Karrie's eyes were misty as she took her dad's hand in hers and whispered, "I love you, Dudd."

They all smiled, and I knew they were sharing an inside joke, something I had no knowledge of, and I felt a weird pang in my chest.

My family didn't have anything like that.

No secret nicknames, or fun family stories. Our father had never given up anything for us, and my mother never looked at him the way Sam looked at Judd. Seeing the three of them together made me realize how lackluster my childhood really was.

Sure, we had money and never wanted for anything material. But, all the money in the world couldn't buy the love these three obviously shared.

It made me uncomfortable. Like I was witnessing something private that I could never understand.

"Excuse me," I managed, my voice rougher than usual.

I pushed back from the table and went to the restroom. After a few minutes, once I'd steeled myself from the emotions I'd been feeling, I washed my hands and went back out into the apartment.

Before returning to the table, however, I made a pitstop at the fridge for a beer.

Realizing I was being selfish and couldn't show up with a drink for myself and nothing for anyone else, I popped my head around the corner and asked, "Would anyone like a drink? Beer? More wine? Water?"

"I'll have another glass," Sam said.

"Beer sounds good," Judd replied.

"Just water for me," Karrie added, her gaze on me showing her concern.

I gave her a small smile to assure her I was fine and went back to grab the drinks. Once everyone had their beverage of choice, I took my seat and picked up my fork.

I can do this.

"Karrie says she has a little brother, Carter, I believe?" I prodded.

"Oh my gosh, Carter," Karrie said, covering her mouth when a disbelieving laugh slipped out. "I didn't even ask about him. Where is he? What a terrible sister."

"He's fine, don't worry about it. He's at your grandparents'," Sam replied.

"He wanted to come with us, but we're planning to hit the casino on the way back home and maybe stay a couple nights," Judd explained.

"Yeah, a sort of mini getaway, just the two of us," Sam agreed, waggling her eyes at her husband.

"Ew, gross," Karrie cried. "Never do that again."

Sam just laughed, and I couldn't stop my lips from quirking up.

Her parents were pretty cool, and, *believe me*, I'd never thought that about anyone's parents before. In my experience, children were to be seen and not heard, and the only thing parents were good for was using you either as a shield or a punching bag.

Physically and verbally.

I watched and listened while they teased each other and joked around, and wondered what life must have been like in Karrie's house growing up.

I mean, I got along well with my brothers now, and I hoped those bonds would continue to grow, but the kind of vibe these three had going on filled me with a longing I didn't understand.

Parents dropping everything to drive hundreds of miles to make sure I was okay? It was unfathomable.

TWENTY-FOUR

KARRIE

Due to my parents' unexpected arrival, not only had Ridge and I not watched Netflix (*had lots of sex*) the night he came to dinner, but I hadn't seen him since.

Don't get me wrong, spending time with my parents was great, especially since I wouldn't see them again until Christmas, but I went to bed every night wishing I knew where things stood with Ridge.

He'd been obviously uncomfortable at dinner, and I wasn't sure if it was because he'd been kind of ambushed, or because meeting them wasn't part of our pact and he wasn't interested in making our relationship *that* real.

"Do you think he didn't like us?" my mom had asked.

I'd shook my head and told her, "He hasn't talked much about it, but I don't think he had a very good childhood, and doesn't get along with his parents. He probably didn't know how to handle our freaky good relationship."

"Aww, I hate that for him," she'd said with a frown.

My mom was a total bleeding heart. As a kid, ours was always the house all the kids hung out at. My parents were the cool parents, the fun ones who always had the best snacks, horror movie nights, and played hide and seek in the dark.

Needless to say, Ridge hadn't spent any more time with them, and we'd decided that he'd go to the game with his brothers, and I'd go with my parents.

I understood, but I was disappointed with how things turned out and found myself really looking forward to the stupid Homecoming party. I wasn't all fired up to hear Crush run his mouth again, but I was excited to see the girls' makeovers, and, more than anything, to see Ridge.

How had he become so important to me in such a short amount of time?

"Okay, baby, you be good and have fun with Ridge over Thanksgiving. Let me know if I need to come up there and teach his mother a lesson," my mom said as she squeezed me tightly.

"I will," I replied with a laugh.

"Love you, Karebear," Judd said when I turned to him.

"I love you, too, Dad. Love you, Mom. You guys have fun and don't do anything illegal at the casino."

"Love you, baby girl. We'll be good," my mom promised.

I waved until I could no longer see their car, then hurried inside to get ready for the big party.

Since this was supposed to be the big reveal, I'd decided to take some extra time and effort into my appearance tonight. Sure, technically Ridge and I weren't part of the competition, but I still wanted to look *transformed* from that first night, and make myself look good for what I was hoping would be a long and satisfying night for both of us.

I picked out the denim skirt and white cropped top I'd picked up on our shopping spree and paired it with gladiator sandals.

But, before putting it on, I washed up, shaved everywhere,

and took the time to give myself a Brazilian blowout and straighten my hair. It took time and patience, which was why I usually chose to let my curls go au natural, but I wanted to do it.

The preparation almost made the anticipation even greater. Like, *I knew* I was prepping myself to *hopefully* be seen by Ridge later, and him having no idea what was coming made me kind of hot.

On the other hand, there was always the chance that I'd be rejected. That he'd still put the brakes on anything other than kissing.

Regardless, I was going to feel my absolute best, and hopefully make his decision, *and him*, really hard.

Wink, wink.

I watched a makeup tutorial and not only did the perfect winged eyeliner, but filled in my eyebrows as well. By the time I was finished, I barely recognized myself in the mirror, and I was ready to make Ridge my bitch.

"*Ho-ly shit!*" Mina called when I walked out.

When she put her fingers in her mouth and whistled loudly, I let out a happy laugh.

She spun her finger to tell me to turn around and exclaimed, "*Caliente!*"

I did a little shimmy for her benefit.

"Are you coming tonight?" I asked her.

"I sure hope so," Mina replied, widening her eyes comically.

"*God*, me too," I agreed with a giggle.

"Sing it sister," she said, giving me a high five, before adding, "But, yes, Trap and I will be going to the party at Delta later ... after the makeover nonsense."

"Cool, well, text me when you're on your way."

"Okay," she said, but when I started for the door, she called, "Wait, how are you getting there?"

"My bike."

Mina came toward me, shaking her head furiously.

"Oh, hell no. There's no way you're showing up at Delta for the biggest party of the year riding a damn bicycle. Plus, you'd flash your coochie to half the population of the college on the ride over."

"Ridge is already there and has to get ready for tonight, so I told him I'd meet him there. It's no big deal," I assured her, although I hadn't thought about the fact that the skirt I was wearing *was* pretty mini and may appear indecent on my bike.

"I'll give you a ride," Mina told me.

Not asked ... told.

"But, you're not ready and I already took too long getting ready. I'm going to miss the big reveals."

"I'll just drop you off and come back to get ready. Don't worry, Princess Karrie, no one will see your frumpy roommate. I won't embarrass you."

I put my hands on her shoulders and looked dead in her face.

"You could never in a million years embarrass me and no one in the world would ever call you *frumpy* ... at least, not to my face. Not if they want to live."

"Easy, *killer*, you don't have to defend my honor, cause I don't give a flying fuck what anyone thinks of me. Now, let's get your sexy ass over to Delta so Ridge can lose his shit."

"*Aww*, Ridge calls me 'killer,'" I said, more eager than ever to get to him.

"Careful," Mina warned. "You're in danger of crossing into *gag me* territory."

"Sorry," I said, playing back what I'd just said in my head and realizing she was right. I needed to tone it down. The last thing I wanted was to revert back to *Drake's Karrie*, who made everything about her man and started to lose herself.

I was never going to be that person again, and, honestly, I didn't think Ridge would want that either.

"No worries. Now, let's get going, because *this look* was meant to be seen."

TWENTY-FIVE
RIDGE

It was early, but the party was already lit.

We'd won the Homecoming game, so everyone had basically started partying at halftime and were still going strong.

This usually meant the party would either fizzle out early, or people'd start getting their second wind and really lose their shit by midnight. The pledges were gonna have a helluva mess on their hands to clean up tomorrow.

Not my problem.

Once I was sure my things and my room were locked up tight, I went downstairs to join the festivities.

"Yo, Ridge," Antoine, our president, called out when I hit the bottom.

I moved to join him, Crush, Papi, and Javi in the living room.

"'Sup?" I said in greeting as I took a seat and accepted the beer a pledge offered.

"That was a great game today," Javi said from his perch on the arm of the couch.

"Yeah, and it's gonna be an even better night," Crush said, shamelessly turning the conversation to himself, as usual. "You won't believe some of these makeovers. I mean, these chicks were low fours at best, and now they're solid eights, maybe even a nine or two."

I ignored him, because, honestly, if I let the shit he said get to me, I'd have beat his ass into the ground years ago.

"How're things going with your girl, man, you ready to take her home?" Papi asked me.

He was the only one of the guys who knew the true nature of my relationship with Karrie, since, after all, the whole thing had been his idea.

I didn't think he asked because he was worried his advice wasn't sound, because *Papi's always right*, but he was actually invested. He believed in the counsel he gave, and liked playing that role in the frat, and truly wanted everything to work out.

"Everything's right on track," I assured him.

"Wait, you're taking that chick home with you? Like, to your actual house ... to meet your family?" Crush asked, obviously flabbergasted.

I guess I couldn't fault him, since it was out of character. Still, that didn't mean I didn't glare at him and ask, "What's it to you?"

He shrugged.

"Nothing really. Although, it was my challenge that brought you two together, so, I guess you should be thanking me for playing Cupid."

"For fuck's sake, not everything's about you," I retorted.

"It is in my world. Just like in your world, everything's about you," he shot back.

"Are you drunk?" I asked him, because what the hell was he talking about.

"Not yet," Crush said, standing up and stretching his arms over his head. "But, I'm about to be. Imma go make sure the mic's all set up. Catch you guys in a bit."

I looked back at the guys and my expression must have shown my frustrations, because Papi laughed and said, "Crush is Crush, man, he's not gonna change anytime soon."

"Dude's a tool," I replied.

"That may be, but he's also a brother," Antoine interjected. "So keep the peace and let the shit he says roll off your back."

"I always do," I began, but before I could finish my thought I heard Wes, who was our greeter for the night, call, "Hey, Karrie, you look beautiful."

I stood up without a word to my brothers, and crossed the room like a man in a trance. When I rounded the corner, the sight of Karrie almost brought me to my knees.

"You look stunning," I murmured, eager to get her in my arms.

I hugged her briefly, but since she obviously spent time on her makeup, I settled for a kiss on the cheek.

For now.

One look at her and I knew tonight there was no way I'd be able to stop at making out, and, if the signals she'd been giving were any indication, she'd be right there with me.

God, I hoped so.

"Thank you, you look pretty hot yourself," Karrie said with a coy smile, which let me know she could see the effect she had on me, and she liked it.

"What, this old thing?" I joked, picking imaginary lint off of my blue Michael Kors shirt.

I'd noticed Karrie liked me in blue, so I'd dressed with her in mind. Looking down at her killer legs and flat stomach, I hoped she'd done the same. As much as I was enjoying the view, I couldn't wait to see what was underneath.

"Want a drink?" I asked, taking her hand and leading her inside.

It was mostly brothers, pledges, and their makeover guests.

The party would go public in another hour, after Crush finished with his self-indulgent speeches and declared the winning pledge and girl.

"Yes, I'd love one," she replied, walking so close her arm brushed against mine, causing my libido to wake up and take notice.

"What's your poison tonight? Beer, Captain and Coke, jungle juice?"

Her lip curled up when she said, "I think I'll skip the jungle juice. Too many germ possibilities. I'll have a Captain."

"Coming right up," I said, before turning to the nearest pledge and ordering, "Captain and Coke ... and don't make it fifty-fifty, one shot is enough."

The pledge nodded and hurried off.

"Thanks, last time they made it pretty strong."

"Yeah, they tend to do that, which works for most of our partygoers. But, I'd like both of us to be fully functional tonight."

Karrie turned into me and grabbed my other hand, so we were standing with our chests flush as she looked up at me.

"I was thinking the same thing," she replied.

"Yeah?" I asked with a grin.

She bit her lower lip and gave a nod of affirmation.

Oh yeah, we are totally on the same page.

TWENTY-SIX

KARRIE

"Oh my gosh, you all look so great," I told the group of women who were all standing around for their moment in the spotlight.

Some looked excited, others nauseous, but they seriously did all look great. The pledges had done a good job with makeover, or, at least the girls were making it look like they did. Who knew what really went on behind closed doors. For all I knew, they could be more like me and Ridge, and have ulterior motives for participating in Crush's event.

"Thanks, so do you," Trixie said. "Not that you didn't look great before."

"Oh, I'll say this is a quite different look than my sweatpants and messy bun," I replied with a laugh. "But, thank you. We should really hang out sometime ... the four of us."

Trixie looked at me funny and shook her head.

"Actually, Wes and I aren't a thing, and after tonight I don't think I'll be around again."

"Sorry, I didn't mean to assume, I thought I saw a spark between the two of you," I said, feeling like an idiot.

"I'm dating someone ... a woman. But, it's not that. I'm bi, and I think Wes is a great guy, it's just this whole scene. It's not for me."

"I get that," I agreed easily. "Delta can be a bit much, especially at things like this, but you and Wes are still friends, right?"

"Probably not after tonight," Trixie said, and then turned and walked away.

I watched after her for a moment, wondering what she meant, and jumped when a pair of strong arms surrounded my waist.

"They're about to start," Ridge said, his breath hot against my ear, causing me to shiver.

"Okay," I replied softly, suddenly wishing we could run upstairs and hide for the rest of the night.

I have a few ideas of how we could stay occupied...

"God, you smell good," he said, and I felt his lips skim the base of my neck.

"I'm glad you like it. After all, you did pick it out," I said with a light laugh.

"Delicious," Ridge growled, and I had to fight the urge to spin around and tackle him to the floor.

"We'd better go," I told him as everyone starting filing into the other room.

He let out a frustrated noise, but took my hand as we followed the group.

"Welcome, everyone," Crush was saying as we entered. "Was that a great game today or what? Now, it's the night you've all been waiting for ... one pledge, and one hot female, will win our makeover challenge. Are you ready to get started?"

I don't know if he was expecting a rousing cheer, but what he received was a reluctant chorus of *yeses*, with one, *I guess*.

Crush didn't let that get him down, though, he kept right on going like he was the MC at Fashion Week.

"First to the stage, we have ... Curtis and Shay!"

As Crush called out their names, the pledges and their "dates" walked on stage and posed briefly before walking back down again. Crush had a slideshow playing that showed the *before* picture of each girl, which helped the judges see what a transformation had been made over the last few weeks.

I was leaned back against Ridge, with his arms around me and my head tucked under his chin.

It was my new favorite place to be.

"And, the winners of this year's makeover challenge are..." Crush did an air drumroll. "Wes and Trixie!"

I clapped and yelled out, "*Whoop!*" while Ridge called out his brother's name.

Wes looked embarrassed, but pleased, and I remembered how Ridge had said getting points and time with the board would look good for him once they were making decisions on who could join, although, I'd think that being Ridge's brother would help him out as well.

Trixie, on the other hand, looked kinda pissed.

The picture behind her showed a pretty girl with long raven hair, wearing jeans and a sweater that was about three sizes too big. Now, her hair was cut into a cute-as-hell pixie, which really showed off her pretty face and long neck. She was wearing a black and red skater dress with combat boots.

Trixie was totally punk rock, which may be why she scowled at Crush when he said, "Trixie, you went from forgettable to fuckable in only a few weeks, which means, you're welcome at Delta any time you want between now and your graduation."

"Crush," Antoine said, holding his hand out for the mic as he walked on the stage.

I guess Crush had taken it too far with the fuckable comment.

I saw Antoine say something to Trixie that the rest of us

couldn't hear, but she simply gave Crush the bird and stormed off stage.

"Sorry about that, ladies, Crush apologizes for his sexist and rude comments. He was not speaking on behalf of Delta. Now, it's time to open the doors and celebrate our Homecoming win. Have a good night and be safe," Antoine said, before gesturing to someone off stage to turn off the mic and get rid of the screen.

"What a dick," I said, turning in Ridge's arms. "I hope Trixie's okay; do you think I should check on her?"

Ridge's arms tightened around me and my body brushed against his. I felt his hardened cock and my body tingled in response.

"Wes went after her," he said, dipping his face close to mine and speaking low, so only I could hear him. "What do you say we skip the rest of the party and go upstairs?"

I lifted up so I could whisper in his ear, "I'd say you must be slippin' cause I've been wanting to go upstairs since I walked in the door."

Ridge moved his mouth to my throat, his teeth scraping the skin and causing me to hold on tight as he replied, "Is that right?"

I made a sound somewhere between *yes* and a desperate gurgle.

"Baby, all you gotta do is ask, and I'll do whatever you want ... always."

Wow, that was a blanket statement I could really get behind.

I pulled back to look up into his eyes, which looked electric thanks to his blue shirt.

"I'm asking," I told him, and his pupils dilated in response.

He took my hand and started to practically drag me to the stairs. I laughed and jogged to keep up, happy, eager, and completely ready to *finally* get him naked.

We'd just reached the base of the stairs when Wes came running over and blocked our path.

"Wes," Ridge said hurriedly, when he got a good look of his brother's face. "What's wrong?"

"Ridge, I need your help ... I think I fucked up."

TWENTY-SEVEN
RIDGE

Wes, Karrie, and I scrambled up the stairs and down the hall to my room.

Once I'd unlocked the door and we'd all rushed inside, I locked it behind us and looked to my brother.

"Talk," I ordered, wondering what in the hell could have him so spooked when minutes ago he was fine.

"Okay ... I followed Trixie out of the house and caught up to her on the street. She's been acting so weird lately, different. When she ran off, I figured she was pissed about Crush, even though he says dumb shit like that all the time. But, when I stopped her, she told me why she'd really agreed to the makeover."

"And," I prodded when he stopped talking. "Why'd she do it?"

"She works for the paper. The school paper. I guess she's a journalism major or something. She said she was looking for her big break and when I asked her about doing the makeover for Delta, she decided to do an expose on pledging ... but it turned into more than that."

"What the fuck did she say, Wes?" I asked when he paused again.

He was pacing back and forth in my room, wringing his hands, so I knew he was freaking out, but I needed to know everything she said.

It was my job to protect the frat.

"She said she's exposing everything ... Crush's treatment of the pledges and the women who come to Delta, the sexist makeover ritual, and who knows what else."

"You had no idea about any of this?" I asked, knowing if it turned out he was part of it, they'd boot him out of the frat, no questions asked.

"No, Ridge, honestly, I didn't," Wes said, his eyes begging me to believe him. "I'd never do that to you, you know that. I told you, when I met Trixie, she agreed to do this if I helped her pick up women. I thought we were friends, and yeah, she started asking lots of questions and stuff, but I assumed it was because she was interested. I asked her about her life, too ... That's what friends do."

Wes sat down on my bed so hard he bounced and put his head in his hands.

"I guess it was all just bullshit. Trixie was using me for her story."

Karrie murmured, "*Aww, Wes*," and moved to sit on the bed next to him. She placed her arm around his shoulder and assured him, "It's not your fault. You liked her and had no reason to think she was lying to you. Hell, she fooled all of us."

"I need to go down and talk to Antoine, let him know what's going down. You good?" I asked Karrie, who looked up at me and nodded, before turning back to Wes.

I exited the room and jogged back down the stairs, muttering expletives under my breath with each step.

I hadn't sensed anything off about Trixie either, so I couldn't really fault Wes for being duped. Still, I tried to think about how what she'd seen and heard could be spun to make us sound like a bunch of misogynistic assholes, and starting swearing louder.

I moved through the crush of people, wondering where the fuck they'd all come from so fast, and beelined toward our president, who was talking to a few other frat presidents in the corner.

Great.

"Ridge, hey, how's it going, man? Congrats to your brother," one of the guys said. I was pretty sure he was the Sigma president, Cody or something.

I nodded and said, "Thanks," before turning to Antoine and asked, "Can I talk to you for a minute, in private?"

Antoine told the guys he'd get with them later and started to follow me. I looked around the packed space, wondering where the best place to talk to him alone would be, and decided to head down the hall to where his bedroom was located, in the back of the house.

"Can we talk in here?" I asked, pointing my thumb toward his door.

He moved past me to unlock it and walked inside.

"What's up?" Antoine asked after I shut us inside.

I glanced around the room to ensure we were alone and said, "Trixie, the girl who entered the contest with Wes and won, is actually an undercover reporter for the school paper. She's writing an exposé on Delta."

Antoine blinked slowly, and I could hear the wheels spinning in his head.

"Do we know what she's writing about, exactly?"

I shook my head and replied, "No one's read anything yet, but she told Wes it would be about Crush, the treatment of our pledges, and the contest."

"How bad, do you think?"

"Well, the last thing Crush said was that shit about her going from forgettable to fuckable, so probably pretty fucking bad."

"Shit ... What about Wes, did he know about it?" he asked, narrowing his eyes at me. "I know he's your brother, but our priority is to Delta. If he's in on it..."

"I know," I said, holding up my hand. "But he wasn't in on it. I'd stake my office on it."

Antoine nodded.

He was a good dude and I'd never given him a reason not to trust me. So, he'd believe me when I said Wes didn't know about Trixie's motives, and I knew my brother well enough to know when he was lying to me. He was telling the truth.

"We need to get ahold of her, see if we can find out what she's written, maybe she can be reasoned with," he said, and I knew my night was not about to be spent in Karrie's arms like I'd initially hoped.

"Got it. I'll grab Wes and take him with me. He'll know how to track her better than me."

"Okay, and, if it looks like her focus is mainly on Crush, see if she'd be willing to keep Delta's name out of it. I've talked to him repeatedly, and let him slide more than I should, and he still doesn't get it. If he's going down for being a prick, there's no reason we need to go down with him. Crush's views are not Delta's and we won't stand by and take the fall for his actions."

I felt a momentary pang of sympathy for Crush, who no doubt expected his brothers to have his back, not hang him out to dry. But, dude was a complete ass and always had been, and no matter what we said, showed no signs of changing. So, I squashed it.

"You got it," I told my president, then went to grab my brother and head out in search of Trixie.

TWENTY-EIGHT
KARRIE

Before they left, Ridge had given me the option to be dropped off at home, or to stay and wait in his room.

I'd opted to wait.

It wasn't just because I'd had my heart set on introducing peen to my vagina, and maybe my mouth, but I was worried about Wes and curious to see what Trixie's response to Ridge would be if he caught up with her.

Up until that night, she'd seemed so genuine, it was hard for me to believe it was all a lie.

After two hours and no updates, I began to get tired. I could still hear the party thumping down below, but I was an expert at blocking noise out and concentrating on one thing, so I'd pulled a well-worn book off of Ridge's shelf to pass the time.

Figuring he wouldn't mind, I borrowed one of his U of M T-shirts so that I could get comfortable.

Once my face was washed, hair was up in a bun, and my sexy clothes were neatly folded on his dresser, I crawled in bed with a novel by James Patterson. I'd never read him before, and hoped to at least find his words entertaining.

I didn't even make it to the second chapter before I dozed off.

I woke up when the mattress depressed and I felt someone slipping under the covers next to me.

"Ridge?" I whispered, eyes still closed.

"Yeah, baby, it's okay, go back to sleep."

"What time is it?" I asked, blinking my eyes open gingerly.

"Late. Like three in the morning," he replied.

I turned on my side so I was facing him and asked, "Did you find her?"

"Yeah, we did. She agreed to keep Delta's name out of it, so that's good. But, the story will run on Monday."

"How's Wes?"

"Pretty pissed. He wouldn't even look at her, at first, but he's the one who convinced her to keep the focus on Crush, not Delta. He'll be okay, he's just feeling like an idiot for getting played."

"It's not his fault."

"I know, but he still feels bad. I hope it's okay, but I told him he could ride back with us for Thanksgiving."

"Of course."

It was quiet for a few seconds, and I realized I could no longer hear noise coming from below.

I wondered if Ridge had fallen asleep when he asked, "Are you wearing my shirt?"

"Mmmhmm, the jean skirt wouldn't have been fun to sleep in," I replied.

My eyes had adjusted to the dark, so I could see Ridge move onto his back, his eyes on the ceiling.

He wasn't wearing a shirt, and I wondered if he had on shorts, underwear, or nothing at all. I mean, I doubted he'd slip into bed naked with me, but the not knowing was causing my blood to stir, cause it *was* possible.

My imagination started working overtime and I visualized myself reaching under the sheets and finding Ridge's hard length waiting for me. I imagined grasping him in my fist and moving it up and down, holding him tighter as I jacked him off.

My nipples pebbled and my body grew warm as I heard the sounds he'd make in my mind.

Maybe he'd beg, which really turned me on, or maybe he'd lose all control and throw me down on the bed so he could fuck me senseless.

I gasped audibly and Ridge's head turned my way.

"You good?" he asked.

God, I wanted to do it. I wanted to be brave and go after what I wanted, but the fear of rejection made me pause.

"Yes, I was just thinking..."

"About what?"

I bit my lower lip and wondered, if I couldn't physically show him what I wanted, could I tell him?

It felt safe in the cloak of dark, so I took a deep breath and answered, "About touching your cock."

Oh my God, I actually said it.

Ridge's eyes widened and he shifted beneath the sheets.

"Really?" he asked, his tone rough.

I nodded.

"Tell me," he urged.

I closed my eyes and searched for my inner vixen.

"Well, first I'd tease the head ... squeeze it a little, but not too hard. Then, I'd wrap my hand around you, like a fist, and move it up and down, from base to tip." I opened one eye to peek at him.

He was watching me intently.

"I bet it feels fucking fantastic," Ridge said, and I knew he wanted me to continue.

"I'd squeeze tighter ... go faster ... and move my other hand to play gently with your balls."

"Yes, I'd like that," he said, voice full of desire. "And, while you're doing that, could I touch you?"

"*Yes*," I whispered, clenching my legs together to try and relieve some of the building pressure.

"Do it, Karrie. *Touch me*. Just like you said..."

TWENTY-NINE
RIDGE

I was so hard there was a chance that one touch from Karrie would make me explode.

It was a chance I was more than willing to take.

Her eyes opened and she released the lip she'd been chewing on as I rid myself of my boxer briefs. She still looked unsure, so I reached for her in the dark, my thumb caressing her swollen lower lip.

Karrie gasped and darted her tongue out to lick my thumb tentatively.

I growled, which made her smile, and *thankfully* gave her the courage to move her hand beneath the sheets to do the things she'd driven me crazy talking about. *Jesus*, hearing her talk about jacking my cock in her sexy, sweet voice had nearly driven me mad.

I'd had to stop myself from attacking her like a lion on a gazelle.

The first brush of her skin on my dick was the sweetest form of torture I'd ever felt. I'd never wanted anyone as much as Karrie, never waited to claim a woman I wanted to fuck, never felt this sting of anticipation.

It made everything so much more pronounced.

Almost like I was a teenager again, feeling the touch of a girl for the first time.

She touched me just as she'd described and I couldn't wait to reciprocate. As soon as she fisted my cock, I moved, eager to have my hands on her. To hear her desire, and feel her silky pussy beneath my fingers.

Karrie kept her grip on me as I explored her body. Starting with her perky breasts and working my way down. I couldn't wait to taste her ... every inch, but first, I was dying to make her feel as good as she was making me feel in that moment.

I pushed her panties down and moved closer. The jostling had her squeezing so as not to lose hold of my dick, and I had to clench my teeth when she pumped me hard and fast.

"Slow down," I urged. "I don't want it to be over before it begins."

"Oh, sorry," Karrie said, loosening her hold.

I shifted so I could lower my face close to hers and said, "Never apologize for touching me like you own me. I fucking love it," before claiming her mouth with mine as I delved into her wet heat.

Karrie arched beneath me and moaned against my lips, and I felt like the king of the fucking world.

"Take my shirt off," I ordered after breaking the kiss.

Doing so meant she had to let go of my dick and scoot up to pull my shirt over her head. While she was doing that, I scooted down on the bed and shoved my face into her cunt.

"*Oh, God,*" she cried, her hands coming to my head, one had pulling my hair tightly.

That was all the encouragement I needed. Shoving my hands under her ass, I lifted her up so I could have better access while keeping her still. I licked and sucked until she was writhing against my mouth, her hips bucking instinctively as she sought her release.

Within seconds, Karrie erupted around me, her grip on my hair deliciously painful, and I sucked until the last of the shocks subsided.

"*Ridge*," she cooed, my name on her lips the most erotic sound.

I eased her back on the bed, kissing her thigh before looking up to see her hands on her breasts and her head turned to the side.

I kissed her stomach, breasts, and throat, before hovering over her completely and saying, "You look so beautiful."

Karrie blushed sweetly, turning to face me as she wrapped her legs around my waist.

Then she uttered the two most wonderful words in the English language ... "*Fuck me.*"

Eager to comply, I jumped off the bed to reach in my dresser and grab the condoms I had stashed there, before hurrying back to join her.

She watched as I pinched the condom, rolling it over the crown and down the length of my cock.

Once I was sheathed, I sat back against the headboard and motioned for her to get on top of me.

"You want me..." Karrie asked, looking a little unsure.

"Have you never done it this way?" I asked, really fucking pleased at the thought.

She shook her head.

"You're gonna love it," I promised.

My dick jumped as I watched her get up and throw her leg over me, then scoot up the bed on her knees, until I felt the heat of her pussy against me.

"Just grab my dick and lower yourself on it, then you can hold onto my shoulders, or reach back and brace against my thighs, whatever feels more comfortable to you. Believe me, there are no wrong answers when it comes to this position."

Karrie nodded, her expression serious, like she was studying for an exam or something.

I lost the ability to speak as she welcomed me into her body slowly, inch by glorious inch, and when she could go no farther, I could no longer think. All I could do was *feel*.

"That feels so nice," Karrie murmured, gripping my shoulders as she began to rock against me.

"Now, lift up like you're gonna move off, but stop right before you lose me, then slam back down ... hard and fast."

Karrie followed my instructions, gliding up and down until I told her to stay down and ride.

Her breath caught as her clit hit my pelvic bone and she began to move faster. I watched her face turn soft and her cheeks redden as her head fell back and eyes closed. Needing to help get her there, I gripped her hips tightly and moved her even faster.

Karrie's lips parted and a low moan came out, just as I felt her walls clench around me.

"*Fuck, yes,*" I groaned, my own pleasure ripping through me like an electric shock.

Our cries mingled in the damp air as I pumped into her and her movements slowed. After a few more thrusts, my vision blurred and Karrie collapsed against my chest.

We stayed like that for a few moments, both struggling to catch our breath and slow our racing hearts.

"That was amazing," Karrie murmured against me. "We should always do that..."

I laughed, happy and completely relaxed, and hugged her tighter.

"We absolutely should," I agreed.

THIRTY
KARRIE

I couldn't stop smiling.

Mina told me it was pretty annoying, but since she was just as happy with Trap, as I was with Ridge, she couldn't even be mad about it.

Ridge and I had spent as much time as we could together since Homecoming.

We'd had tons of sex ... oral sex, semi-public sex, Kama Sutra sex ... seriously, all the sex.

My body was so sore, it felt like I'd been training for a marathon or something, which, I guess I had. *Marathon sex.*

Now, we were on our way to his family's estate ... *yeah, estate* ... in Chicago for Thanksgiving. The goal we'd been working toward since we met was finally here, and it was crazy how things had changed in such a short amount of time.

I know it all started as a ruse, but now that we were actually on the way to meet his family, I was actually hoping they'd like me.

I didn't want to pretend to be someone I wasn't, I wanted to go in there as Ridge's actual girlfriend and talk to his mom just like I would in any normal situation. Sure, there'd be nerves, but I was really looking forward to seeing this side of Ridge.

The only problem was, we hadn't really discussed this trip.

Other than the initial breakdown of expectations, Ridge hadn't said anything new about what was going to happen. All he'd done was remind me to pack the more conservative items I'd bought.

Which was fine.

I knew his family was more Vineyard Vines than Forever 21, and by the way he and Wes were dressed for the drive down, in khakis and Polos, *even though it would take hours to get there*, I figured they were playing a part, just like I was.

That didn't mean that Ridge would be embarrassed to introduce me, as I really was, to his family ... *right?*

Of course not.

I'd straightened my hair again, and had on a long-sleeved striped knit dress and flats, rather than the sweats and comfy tee I'd normally travel in.

It was all a part of the plan, and I was okay with it, *really*. So, I'd be uncomfortable for the long weekend, no big deal. Ridge was worth it. The extra time it took to get ready, the straight-laced clothes. He'd been honest with me from the beginning about what this trip was.

"Have you heard from Mom?" Ridge asked, speaking for the first time in an hour and startling me.

I turned around to see if Wes had heard him when he didn't reply, and saw him sacked out in the backseat.

"He's asleep," I told Ridge.

"Of course he is," he said with a sigh. "Wes has always been that way. In the car for five minutes, and he's out. Before the plane even taxies down the runway ... slumped. The guy can sleep anywhere."

After a few minutes of silence, I asked, "Are you okay?"

Ridge glanced at me, then back at the road.

"Yeah, I'm good. The ride home always makes me tense, because although I have an idea of what to expect when I get there, my parents sometimes surprise me by being even bigger assholes than I remember."

"I'm sorry," I said, lamely. I couldn't fathom not having a good relationship with my parents.

"At least my dad won't be there ... and I look forward to seeing Brody."

"What's he like?"

"Brody? I don't know. He's still seventeen, and I've been at college for most of his high school years, but he's always been a good kid. He's probably the most easy-going out of all of us, being the youngest, and he's never had a hard time making friends."

"I can't wait to meet him," I said, wondering if he was more like Ridge or Wes. "And, other than Brody and us, it'll just be your mom?"

"Yup. Dad moved out, so it's Brody and Mom at home. Poor guy. I couldn't imagine being the only one at home with her, stuck being the sole focus of her attention. Especially now that Dad's not there to be her verbal punching bag."

"What's she like?"

"Mommy dearest?" he asked with a sneer. "Pretentious, judgmental, oblivious ... pick a nasty descriptor and you've got Susan Temple."

"Quit talking shit," Wes piped in sleepily. "You always see the worst in her."

"And you only see the best. It's like you have blinders on, Wes. I don't know how you can still stick up for her," Ridge shot back, glaring at his brother in the rearview mirror.

"Because if I don't, then who does she have? No one. Dad's

always treated her like shit, you hate her, and Brody's started to act like she doesn't exist."

"Sounds like Mom talking, not you."

"Yeah, well, I'm the only one who'll talk to her, so what am I supposed to do?" Wes asked angrily. "She's our mother, Ridge, the only one we'll ever have."

"Unfortunately," Ridge replied, glancing at me again and saying, "She's had so much plastic surgery, I doubt anything on her is original parts. She's always been focused on her career, and not that into being a mom. She's surprised that my dad left her for a younger woman, even though *she* was the other woman when he was married to our sisters' mom."

"Jesus, Ridge, why don't you let Karrie make up her own mind, rather than filling her head with your venom?"

"What, you want to let Karrie walk in there like a lamb to slaughter? She needs to know what she's dealing with ... Look, just go in there like a Stepford wife and you'll be fine."

I saw Wes shake his head before I turned around in my seat and looked out the passenger side window.

If Ridge was expecting me to be a Stepford wife, maybe I'd been wrong. Maybe while I'd been thinking everything had changed between us, and me meeting his family was real, he was going by the terms of the pact.

Maybe nothing had changed at all, and I'd simply got caught up in the fantasy.

THIRTY-ONE
RIDGE

My shoulders were tense and my disposition was one hundred percent asshole.

Coming home did not bring out the best in me.

I was braced and ready for a fight. Maybe I shouldn't be, maybe Wes was right and our mother would be the picture of welcome and acceptance. *Ha!* Yeah, right, and maybe that squirrel climbing the tree in our front yard would suddenly pop up on two legs and offer me coffee.

Could happen.

I tried to offer Karrie a smile of encouragement, but was sure it came out more like a grimace when she simply blinked at me in response.

"Ready?" I asked her. When she nodded I said, "Just let me do the talking."

We left our bags in the car, we had people who'd get them later, and I let Wes lead us into the house. Susan would actually be happy to see him, so I figured it might get us off on the right foot and be a positive start to the weekend.

I couldn't have been more fucking wrong.

"Hey, Mom," I heard Wes say as I walked in and shut the door behind us.

There she was, Susan Temple in all of her glory. Her blonde hair perfectly coiffed, clothes wrinkle free, and the usual bitter beer face expression.

She hugged Wes and said, "Hello, darling. How was your trip?"

"Not bad. I slept most of the way."

She laughed lightly. "Of course you did. Why don't you come into the drawing room?"

She glanced briefly at me before her sharp gaze landed on Karrie. It was apparent, after looking her up and down, that Susan found Karrie wanting, because she didn't bother to hide it. Her face was pinched when she turned her attention back to me and found me still standing near the front door, hands in my pockets like I didn't give a fuck.

"Take your hands out of your pockets, Ridge, this isn't the hallway of your old high school," she said, then turned and walked into the drawing room with Wes.

I moved up next to Karrie and placed my hand on her lower back as we followed them.

"Mom, this is Karrie. She goes to U of M with me. Her family's in shipping," I said as we entered the room to see her and Wes seated on one of the couches.

I felt Karrie stiffen at the lie and wanted to pull her to me and assure her everything was fine. To explain once again that I didn't give a shit about my mother's opinion, but I couldn't give my mother any ammunition to use against us.

I knew Mom and I were in the middle of a standoff even if it wasn't apparent to anyone else. It was always the way with us. She'd pretend I didn't exist and I'd pretend her indifference didn't affect me.

"Yes," she said finally, looking away from Wes. "Your brother told me you were bringing your latest harlot."

I clenched my jaw and looked to Wes, whose jaw had dropped.

"Mom, I said no such..."

"This doesn't concern you, Wesley," she said, flicking her wrist at him, indicating he should butt out. "This is about your brother's lack of respect for me and our home."

"First of all, calling Karrie a harlot is rude, and ridiculous, coming from you. Second, since when is it disrespectful to bring a guest home?"

"Watch your tone with me, *son*. Just because your father is off embarrassing himself with his *other woman*, doesn't mean you can speak to me in that way."

"That's rich, coming from *the original* other woman. You really think now is the time for you to start parenting me and give me lessons in etiquette? Now that I'm in my twenties?"

She stood swiftly and crossed to me and I felt the slap before it landed, almost like a phantom reminder from my childhood.

Karrie gasped in horror from beside me.

My expression bored, I watched the regret flit across my mother's face.

I saw Brody enter the fray from the corner of my eye, but my gaze never left my mother's.

"Did that make you feel better?" I asked dryly, feeling as ugly as my words. "I guess I shouldn't be surprised that you'd resort to violence. After all, you spent my childhood shielding Wes and Brody, but allowed Dad to beat my ass whenever he got the urge."

"*Oh my God*," I heard Karrie cry softly from behind me, her voice full of tears.

Wes got up and moved to her. I could hear him murmuring

softly, but couldn't make out what he was saying. I was sure Karrie was shocked and appalled by what was happening before her, but I was too caught up to stop what was happening and offer her comfort.

This moment was a long time coming.

"Why *was* that, Mom?" I asked, ignoring the look of devastation on my mother's face. "Why'd you care enough about Wes and Brody to shield *them* and not me? Was I not good enough? Or was I expendable since you had two other sons? What did I ever do to deserve Dad's wrath and your indifference?"

I was so angry I was practically shouting, my fists clenched at my sides, and I wondered if this was what my father felt like before he lost control and took his anger out on me.

"It wasn't like that," she said, struggling to regain her composure. God help us if Susan Temple wasn't perfectly controlled. "Your father was trying to teach you how to be a man, like his father had before him. There was nothing I could do."

"Really? Is that what you told yourself so you could sleep at night?" I seethed. "He never laid a finger on my sisters or brothers ... did they not have lessons to learn? Was I so defective I needed extra discipline?"

My mom shook her head and I saw the moment she found her cloak. It was like a steel trap of denial slammed down over her body. Her stance became rigid and her face void of all expression.

"You're overreacting, as usual, Ridge. Your father isn't here to defend himself, and I have somewhere to be, so we'll have to agree to disagree and leave it at that," she said, crossing to the table and picking up her purse.

"Where are you going?" Wes asked.

I shifted to see he had one arm wrapped around Karrie, who was looking at me with eyes full of sorrow.

"The MacAlisters have invited me to their lake house for

Thanksgiving. Once you informed me of Ridge's little power play, bringing this girl here rather than going along with *my* plans for the weekend, I decided to take them up on the offer."

"Seriously, you're leaving? Are we supposed to have Thanksgiving alone?" he asked incredulously, and a dry laugh escaped me at the proof that he actually still wanted to spend time with her.

"I'm sure the staff will keep you well fed, or you could always make reservations at one of those *buffets* ... whatever fits your needs," she said, looking haughtily at Karrie, as if she were the only person in the room who'd eat a holiday meal at a buffet.

She started past me, toward the door, her heels clicking on the hardwood. Once she'd reached the threshold, I turned slightly to look at her and said, "This is the last time I'll step foot in this house."

My mother glanced over her shoulder at me. "So be it," she said, and walked out.

The breath left my body and suddenly everything hurt.

"Sorry, man," Brody said, coming toward me. "She just told me about her change of plans this morning, and I tried to call you guys and give you a head's up on her mood, but no one answered."

"Ridge," Wes began, but I held up my hand to stop him from speaking.

I couldn't listen if he was going to defend her again. Not right then.

"I called Dru, she and the sisters are getting together for a big feast and said we were welcome to come down. I told them we'd be there by nine tonight. She said we can either stay with them or in the apartment over Three Sisters. You up for another road trip?" Brody asked.

I nodded and said, "I just need a couple minutes," before leaving the three of them and walking to the back of the house.

THIRTY-TWO
KARRIE

I was shaking.

I'd never witnessed anything like what had just transpired between Ridge and his mom. My heart was breaking for him, and I was filled with such anger at not only what I'd seen, but what I'd heard.

Ridge's father had abused him ... and his mother knew about it and didn't stop it?

It was such a complete difference from the way I'd been raised, that it almost didn't compute. My heart wanted to deny such a thing was possible, even though I'd just seen it with my own eyes.

First, I'd been devastated that he'd lied about my family, but the more they spoke to each other, the more I realized none of this had anything to do with me, not really. When he'd asked me to come here with him to be a sort of buffer and stop his mother from setting him up with some debutant she wanted him to marry, I'd thought it was kind of funny.

You know, some poor little rich guy problem that would be no skin off my back, especially if I got back at Drake in the process.

But, that scenario was just a drop in the fucked-up bucket of his family life.

"Should we go after him? See if he's okay?" I asked Wes, who still had his arm around me, as if trying to shield me from the vileness of the scene we'd just witnessed.

"No, he needs to be alone to cool down. He'll come back when he's ready, then we'll get out of here, yeah?"

I nodded, thinking, *yes, please, let's get the hell out of here*.

"Uh, hey, I'm Brody, by the way. You must be Karrie."

Brody had a boyish charm. Not as put together as Ridge, but you could already tell his tousled good looks and easygoing smile were going to slay the girls at U of M.

I accepted his outstretched hand and shook it, returning his smile.

"Nice to meet you."

"Sorry about the drama," he said sheepishly.

"It's okay," I replied, looking over his shoulder to where Ridge disappeared, hoping he was okay. "Actually, I'm going to see if I can find him."

Although I realized his brothers knew him better than I did, it didn't feel right for him to be off on his own, upset ... maybe even devastated. I had to go and see if he was okay and offer him comfort, if he'd accept it.

"He'll either be out back, or in his room ... straight back, third door on the left," Brody offered, and I smiled at him in thanks.

I glanced around the house, taking in the antique furniture, art on the walls, and crystal chandeliers that probably cost more than my tuition, but I kept my hands firmly to my sides, just in case I got the urge to touch.

The last thing I needed to do was break something in this museum of a house.

As I passed a large window, I looked outside, but when I didn't see Ridge, I continued toward his bedroom.

When I reached the third door on the left, I noticed it was slightly ajar and knocked softly, before pushing it open to see Ridge standing in the center of the room, with his back to me.

"*Ridge*," I called softly.

The depression of his shoulders had me crossing to him and wrapping my arms around his waist.

Before I could lay my head against his back, he turned and hugged me to his chest.

"I'm sorry," I told him, hating the fact that his mother treated him that way. That both his parents had obviously mistreated him his whole life. "They don't deserve you."

I felt him chuckle lightly and kiss the top of my head.

"I'm sorry you had to see that," Ridge said with a heavy sigh. "I knew she wouldn't be happy, but the worst I expected was cold indifference, not a complete meltdown. I never should have brought you here."

"Hey, it's okay," I assured him, pulling back so I could look up at his face.

He looked like the weight of the world was resting on his shoulders, and I wished I could ease his burden.

"You don't have to worry about me, I can handle it," I added.

"Thank you," Ridge said, lowering to brush his lips across mine.

"For what?" I whispered, rubbing his lower back.

"For being here, for not running screaming after what just happened out there, and for coming after me."

"Anytime," I said, resting my head on his chest and giving him one more big hug, before letting him go and looking around. "What were you doing in here?"

"Actually, I was looking around, seeing if there was anything

I needed to pack and take with me to school. I was being completely honest when I said I never want to come back here. Luckily, they don't control my money, it's in a trust from my grandparents, so I really don't need them for anything," he said, rubbing his hand over his face. "There's nothing for me here but bad memories."

"Okay, do you need help packing?" I asked.

"No," he said, shaking his head as he looked around the room. "There's nothing I want in here."

I glanced around, taking in the trophies, the large sailboat painting, and the assortment of visors hanging from a rack.

"Probably for the best," I told him, fighting back a grin despite the ache for him in my heart. "Looks like a douche lived here."

Ridge let out a bark of laughter.

"You're right, one did," he agreed, before pulling me back into his arms and making me melt by saying, "But you make me want to be better than that guy."

"You don't need to change who you are, just keep being you." I tiptoed up to kiss the corner of his mouth. "Cause, I think you're pretty great."

He kissed me sweetly, then said, "What do you say we get the hell out of here?"

"Let's do it."

Ridge took my hand in his and led me out of the room.

"Sorry about having to do another road trip, but we'll be much happier at my sisters' ... They're not assholes."

I laughed and smiled up at him.

"Actually, I'm excited to meet them."

"They're gonna love you," Ridge promised. "The *real* you, not Stepford Karrie whose family's in shipping."

"You mean Nirvana fan club, Karrie?"

"That's the one," he said, smiling and looking lighter than when I'd found him.

A surge of happiness rushed through me, with the knowledge that *I* was the one who helped him feel better.

THIRTY-THREE
RIDGE

We'd ended up being on the road later than expected and grabbed a hotel room, rather than driving all the way down in one trip. Since we had time, we'd slept in a bit and grabbed breakfast, before getting in the car and finishing the journey.

Walking into my sister Tasha's house was a completely different feeling than walking into my childhood home.

Rather than tension, there was joy.

We'd only met our sisters a few times, but we'd all felt an instant connection. A bond. The three of them were very different, just like my brothers and me, but at their core, they were kind, compassionate, and extremely family-oriented.

I was proud to introduce Karrie to them, and them to Karrie.

"Thanks for setting this up, bro," I told Brody as we entered the living room.

Tasha and Jericho's place was an open concept, so we could see everyone coming down to greet us.

There was lots of laughter and hugs as we said hello.

Since our sisters were all either married or about to be, we not only gained three sisters, but three brothers, a niece, and grandparents. Our family had gotten a whole lot bigger, and I hadn't really appreciated it until now.

"It's so nice to meet you, Karrie," Millie was saying. "This is Jackson, my husband, and Kayla, our daughter."

Karrie already looked right at home, completely at ease amidst strangers. But, I guessed this group was much more like her own family, so she was probably more comfortable in this situation than I was.

I hadn't grown up with big family holidays and game nights, but I was starting to see my brothers and I had been missing out by not having them growing up.

"And, I'm Dru," Millie's twin, Druscilla, said. They were fraternal, but looked a lot alike with their tanned complexion and dark hair that matched ours. "That's Mick, and his mom, Dottie," she added, pointing to the pair who were standing just off to the side.

Mick was a PI and the one who'd found our father for Dru, and was the catalyst in getting us all together. He was built like an MMA fighter, and was a little rough around the edges, but he was a great guy and he obviously loved our sister.

"Hi, Karrie, I'm Jericho, welcome to our home. That gorgeous woman blooming with child is my wife, Natasha. We're so happy to have you."

Karrie blinked up at Jericho, and I could tell she was a little struck by his good looks.

"Calm down, killer," I said, leaning close so only she could hear me. "He's married and about to be a father."

Karrie flushed and slapped my arm.

"Thanks so much for inviting me," Karrie replied when she finally found her voice.

Jericho just grinned down at her, then moved to help Tasha, the youngest of the sisters, to the couch. She was very pregnant and eased down to the cushion with a happy sigh, then tilted her head back so Jericho could kiss her.

It wasn't a peck either; no, once their lips touched, it was like they forgot we were here.

"Get a room," Jackson called out good-naturedly.

"Would you like something to drink?" Dru asked as we all started to disburse and relax.

"*God*, yes, something strong," I said, thinking a drink sounded great after the day I'd had.

"*Ridge Temple!*"

Shit!

I was already wincing when I turned to face Dottie, Mick's mom, who was glaring up at me from the recliner she was sitting in.

"Yes, ma'am?" I answered, hoping my respectfulness would win her over.

"Did I just hear you take the Lord's name in vain? Is that how you act on Thanksgiving?"

"No, ma'am?"

She huffed.

"Cursing on Thanksgiving and no hug for Dottie," she muttered loudly under her breath, and I heard Karrie giggle beside me. "It's like we're strangers..."

"Sorry, Dottie," I replied, lowering myself down to give her a hug and kiss on the cheek.

Dottie patted my cheek, looked around to see if anyone was listening, and whispered, "All will be forgiven if you bring me some of those hot Funyons. Hide them in one of those red solo cups or something."

"Coming right up," I assured her with a grin.

"That's a good lad," she said, before looking at Karrie and waving her over. "Come here so I can get a look at ya."

I left Karrie in Dottie's hands and went grab her Funyons

from the kitchen.

"Ma's not giving you a hard time, is she? Her heart's in the right place," Mick said, handing me a glass with amber liquid.

"Thanks. And, no, she's great," I replied, then moved so my back was to Dottie so she couldn't hear what I was saying. "It's okay if I get her the hot Funyons, right?"

Mick chuckled.

"Yeah, don't worry about it, man. She just likes to feel like she's getting away with something."

I nodded, grabbed a cup, and started filling it with the hot Funyons, which looked really out of place on the counter that was overflowing with amazing dishes of Thanksgiving food, so I knew they were probably there for Dottie.

My sisters ran a catering business and small shop. Millie was their cook, and her food was some of the best I'd ever had ... and, I'd dined in more five-star restaurants than I could count.

My stomach growled as I thought about the feast to come.

"Here you go, Dottie," I said as I handed her the cup.

She smiled happily, looking around again before covertly popping a Funyon in her mouth.

"I hope you're all hungry, because it's time to eat," Dru called out.

"*Yes!*" Brody exclaimed, making our sisters laugh happily.

"I could eat that whole turkey," Wes agreed.

"You guys eat as much as you like," Millie said, obviously pleased that we were here.

When Brody had initially told us we had older sisters, I'd been skeptical about meeting them. I hadn't seen the point in meeting women who shared our blood, but were virtual strangers.

Now, I was so glad my brothers had overruled me and forced me to let my guard down, because I was grateful to have them in my life.

THIRTY-FOUR
KARRIE

Ridge's family was amazing.

His parents not included, of course ... but, everyone else ... perfect. Wes and Brody, his sisters, their men, Dottie, seriously, they were the best. They reminded me of my family in the best possible way and made missing my family Thanksgiving a little more bearable.

And, could I just give a personal shout out to Jericho? *Holy buckets!* He was the most gorgeous man I'd ever seen in real life. At first I couldn't even speak, only look at him and drool. I wasn't even embarrassed that Ridge caught me. Tasha was one lucky woman.

To make matters worse, he was totally sweet, one-hundred percent in love with his wife, and cooed sweetly to the baby in her belly.

It was almost more than a person could handle.

Crushing over Jericho aside, the dinner had been amazing. The food was great and everyone spent the night talking and laughing. Dottie was a hoot and Jackson's daughter Kayla was a sweetheart.

We'd all stayed at Tasha and Jericho's, with Ridge and Wes

in one spare room, me in the other, and Brody on the couch. They'd said Ridge and I could share a room, but I didn't feel right about sleeping in the same bed in his sister's house, so the brothers had agreed to the arrangement.

I'd felt bad about Brody getting the couch and offered to switch, but he wouldn't hear of it.

Brody had to get back to study for finals, and Wes was eager to check in at U of M and see if there was any blowback from Trixie's article. There was going to be a board meeting on Sunday, where they were going to discuss whether or not Crush needed to step down as VP and maybe have to leave Delta all together.

I knew Wes felt guilty about it, although Ridge had assured him it wasn't his fault.

So, with all of that going on, we were cutting our holiday short and leaving Tasha's after breakfast. Once Ridge had told them of our plans last night, Millie and Dru had insisted on meeting up for breakfast, so they could all get a little more time together.

I'd gotten up early, so I was already showered, packed, and ready, while the boys were still getting going.

I took my stuff out to the living room to find Tasha, Dru, and Mille all sitting around the table having coffee.

"Good morning," I said, setting my bag by the door before going to join them.

"Morning," Millie said.

"Grab yourself a cup," Tasha added with a smile.

Dru just lifted her mug in greeting.

Once I had fixed my coffee with cream and sugar, I pulled out a chair and joined them.

"The boys still asleep?" Millie asked.

"Brody's in the shower, Wes is still sleeping, but I think Ridge is waiting to get the shower next," I replied.

"So, we have you to ourselves for a little while," Tasha said gleefully.

Uh-oh, I thought, but replied, "Looks like."

"Oh goody."

"So," Millie began, "we learned about your family, school, and softball. Now, how about you tell us about you and Ridge."

"Yeah, how'd you meet?" Tasha asked.

"Well, we met at his frat house. My roommate, Mina, and I went there for a party and he was holding up a wall."

"Holding up a wall?" Dru asked, still looking sleepy.

"Leaning against it," I explained. "He's a professional wall leaner ... All kidding aside, we started talking that night and hit it off."

"And then?" Tasha prodded.

I wasn't sure what more I could say without telling a lie, and I found I really didn't want to lie to his sisters. After everything, I really liked them, and since my feelings for Ridge were true, I didn't see the point in keeping up the ruse.

"Can I be honest with you?" I asked.

Millie nodded seriously and said, "Always."

So, I told them the truth.

I told them about Drake, Ridge's plan for Thanksgiving, the makeover ... *All of it*.

"So, your whole relationship is fake?" Dru asked.

"We agreed to help each other out. To pretend to be dating and participate in the makeover to get back at Drake and get Ridge's mom off his back about getting married to some debutante he has no interest in."

I took a sip of my coffee, and after a few seconds of them watching me closely, I decided I'd come this far, might as well tell them all of it.

"But, somewhere along the way, it stopped being fake and became very, *very* real. Ridge is amazing," I said, unable to hold back my smile. "He's sweet and funny, and knows his own worth. And, he's really helped me do the same. I have fun with him and he makes me feel like the only girl in the world when I'm with him."

"You love him," Millie stated.

"I really do," I agreed with a disbelieving laugh. "I thought I was in love with Drake, but after being with Ridge, I know it must have been a crush or infatuation, because what I feel for Ridge is ... *everything*."

Millie sighed and rested her face on her hand, her expression dreamy.

"I love that," she said. "I can tell he loves you, too. I'm so happy for you both."

"Yeah, I mean, we don't know him that well," Tasha admitted. "But, I've never seen him act the way he does with you. He's obviously very happy."

My cheeks were hurting from smiling so much, but I felt relief. Telling them the truth was the right thing. Now that I'd admitted to myself and his sisters I was in love with him, it was time to tell Ridge the truth, too.

I just prayed they were right and he felt the same way about me.

THIRTY-FIVE
RIDGE

"So, your whole relationship is fake?" I heard Dru ask as I was coming down the hall.

I paused, shocked.

Did Karrie tell my sisters about our pact?

I waited in the hallway, holding my breath as I waited to hear Karrie's response.

"We agreed to help each other out," she replied, and I felt a vice squeeze my heart. "To pretend to be dating and participate in the makeover to get back at Drake and get Ridge's mom off his back about getting married to some debutante he has no interest in."

Anger and hurt filled me and I couldn't stand there and listen anymore. I didn't want to hear my sisters' disappointment over our lies, and I couldn't stand to hear Karrie admitting what we had was nothing more than a game.

I spun on my heels and went back to the room I was sharing with Wes.

Luckily, the room was empty, so I shut the door quietly behind me and leaned against it. I felt an unnatural prick behind my eyes and a pain in my gut I'd never felt before.

"What did you expect?" I muttered to myself, too upset to care that I was speaking out loud. *"You learned a long time ago not to let people in ... They always fucking let you down."*

I think that's what hurt the most ... I didn't expect Karrie to be like everyone else. I'd trusted her, thought she was a straight shooter, and let her get too close. When, in reality, she was just like everyone else.

I sat on the bed, letting the emotion seep out of my, before closing it off and saying, *"That's enough."*

If Karrie wanted to continue with the pact we'd made, and end it when we got back, I'd oblige, just like we'd planned. In fact, I'd make sure everyone knew we were over, and maybe things could go back the way they used to be.

Before I'd met Karrie.

I'd go back to the Delta life I'd cultivated over the last few years, and she could go back to sweatpants and crying over Drake.

"Hey, you good?" Wes asked as he walked in rubbing a towel over his wet hair.

"Yeah, just ready to go," I replied, standing to put all my shit in my bag and make the bed for Tasha.

"Okay," he said, watching me warily. My brothers were no strangers to my temper, and knew to give me space to calm down. I wasn't the type to want to talk about *my feelings*, or what was going in my head. I preferred to work shit out on my own. Knowing this, Wes added, "I'll let Brody and Karrie know we're heading out."

"Thanks."

Ten minutes later, we'd said goodbye to my sisters, who were disappointed we weren't staying for breakfast, and were loading up my car. Millie wouldn't let us go empty-handed, so we also had to-go cups of coffee, muffins, and breakfast burritos to nosh on the way.

"Bro, will you sit up front and keep a good playlist going? I need something to keep me awake," I asked my brother, not looking at Karrie.

"You bet," Brody replied.

I was relieved when Karrie climbed in the back with Wes and Brody took his spot next to me up front.

I brushed off any attempts the three of them made to engage me in conversation, so they eventually gave up and talked amongst themselves, which was good. I was too busy stewing in disappointment to care.

I just wanted to get home and work on forgetting the last few weeks of my life ever happened.

We dropped off Brody, and after a few attempts at talking, Karrie settled back against the seat and dozed off. Wes, of course, slept almost the entire trip. Once we made it back to town, I dropped off a confused Karrie with nothing more than a *have a good night*, before heading to Delta.

"You pissed at Karrie?" Wes asked once he'd moved to the front seat.

I shrugged and figured the cat was about to be out of the bag anyway, so may as well let him in on it.

Karrie obviously didn't care about keeping our secret any longer.

"It was all bullshit," I told him as I pulled onto my street. "We hooked up for the makeover, like you and Trixie, only I wanted her to come home and get Mom off my back and she wanted to use me to make Drake jealous. Now that we've done that, it's over. We'll stage a fake breakup and shit will go back to normal."

"Huh, really? Well, you sure had me fooled. I thought you two were really into each other."

"Nope, it was all totally fake."

Wes seemed like he wanted to say more, but I quickly parked and hopped out of the car.

"Guess I'll walk back to the dorms," he said sarcastically.

"Later," I replied, because honestly, I was having a hard time giving a fuck about anything.

"Yo, Ridge, didn't expect you back already."

I walked in to see some of my brothers, including Papi and Javi, sitting around the table playing poker. There were empty beer cans on the floor, cigars being smoked, and a few Delta groupies hanging around wearing barely any clothes.

"What are y'all up to?" I asked, heading to the bar to pour myself a shot.

"Kind of a makeshift strip poker," Javi replied. "We are on teams with the girls, only we're playing cards and they're taking off an article of clothing if their team member loses. Wanna join?"

"Yeah, sounds good to me," I said, pulling up a chair and fitting it in while they scooted over to make room.

"Yo, Carla!" Javi shouted toward the kitchen. "Get out here and be Ridge's teammate."

"Coming," I heard a female voice reply.

I slammed back my shot and said, "Deal me in."

THIRTY-SIX
KARRIE

Ridge was acting really strange. He'd barely spoken on the entire trip home and he hadn't answered my texts or calls.

I knew he was upset over what happened with his mother, but he'd seemed to be okay once we were with his sisters.

Brody had told me not to stress too much. He said Ridge had always internalized things, and that's how he coped with the issues he had growing up with his parents. Brody figured after all that shit went down with Susan, Ridge probably had a lot to work out.

So, I was trying to be understanding and give him space.

Still, I couldn't help but feel like he was shutting me out ... maybe even pushing me away.

The fact was, this was the first serious problem we'd encountered together, so I didn't know what was the right, or wrong, thing to do. I'd decided to check in and let him know I was thinking about him, without being too overbearing about it.

I gave him two days, and then I figured it was time for me to go over to his place and try and see if he'd talk to me.

I missed him, and wanted to be there for him.

Mina said Delta was having a small party after their board meeting, so she and I were going to go together. She was planning to meet up with Trap, so it all worked out. But, when we arrived, Delta house was bursting at the seams with co-eds.

"Wait, it's Sunday, right?" I asked, wondering why everyone was out partying when school started back up tomorrow.

"Yup," Mina replied. "Looks like everyone needed to blow off some steam after spending the long weekend with their family. I know I do."

"Makes sense," I muttered, even though it really didn't to me.

I looked down at my jeans, T-shirt and cardigan with a sigh. I hadn't really been expecting to be on display in front of a lot of people. Hopefully Ridge and I could hide in his room, rather than be with the crowd.

We walked inside and I was about to head right upstairs, when Ridge's laugh had me turning toward the living room.

He was in the middle of the crowd shot gunning a beer while they cheered him on.

"What in the world?" I asked, stopping a few feet away and waiting while he finished, before calling, "Ridge!"

His head swung toward me and he looked momentarily sad, before his expression morphed into a scowl. Pushing the empty can into a pledge's hand, he stumbled a little bit before finding his footing and crossing to me.

"We doing this now?" he asked oddly.

"Doing what?" I asked, my hands going out to steady him and hopefully get him to come with me.

Suddenly he yelled, *"You know what,"* startling me and my hands fell to my sides.

"Ridge, why are you shouting?" I asked, looking around to see everyone starting to look our way.

"You got what you wanted, now get the fuck out and leave me

alone," he continued, and it was suddenly silent in the house, the only sounds Ridge's heavy breathing and my pounding heart.

"What are you talking about?" I asked, utterly confused.

I felt someone grasp my hand and looked down to see Mina had come up beside me and was watching Ridge with a hardened expression.

"You were only using me to get back at that asshole, Drake. What did you think, I'd be too pussy-whipped to figure it out? I saw the way you were looking at him..."

My eyes widened and filled, and although it dawned on me that he was fake breaking up with me in the terms of our pact, I didn't understand why.

Hadn't things changed between us? Does he not feel the same way I do?

My throat closed tightly as I tried to figure out what to do.

"Come on, Ridge, don't do this, let's go upstairs," I said, reaching out and grabbing his hand.

He whipped his hand away and stumbled back.

"No, I'm done listening to you. It's *over*. You're free to get back together with that shithead, just leave me alone and *never* come back."

Ridge turned around and I was already stepping forward to go after him, when he grabbed onto a beautiful scantily clad girl and pulled her close. It was Caitlyn, the girl from the dressing room.

She was tall, gorgeous, and everything I wasn't. She was beautiful, well-dressed, and exactly the kind of girl Ridge's mom would probably love. High class with just a hint of sex, Caitlyn was the opposite of the cute, softball-playing tomboy I was.

I knew it was all for show, that we'd agreed this was always the way things were going to end. Even as I watched Caitlyn look over her shoulder and smile smugly at me as

Ridge pulled her out of sight, I didn't believe it was actually happening.

"Let's go," Mina said, pulling me backwards.

I let her take me out of the room numbly, but when she would have kept pulling me outside, I dug in my heels.

"No, I need to talk to him, I'm going to go wait up in his room," I told her.

"Karrie, no, *fuck* him. You don't need to hear anything else he has to say."

"I do ... It's okay. *I'm* okay."

"Yeah, and what if he takes that chick up to his room and you're in there? What are you gonna do? Watch?"

"I'll handle it," I assured her, even though I wasn't sure I could.

Mina sighed, but I knew she was giving in.

"Text or call if you need me. I'm not leaving Delta until I hear from you."

"Got it," I said, giving her a quick hug and adding, "Thank you," before running up the stairs.

I put the code in and unlocked Ridge's door, then stepped inside without bothering to turn the light on.

Not even five minutes later, Ridge pushed the door open and came barreling inside.

Alone.

He flipped the light on and swiveled, his eyes narrowing when he saw me sitting in the chair.

"What was that?" I asked him.

"Break up," Ridge replied with a shrug.

"Was *that* really necessary?" I asked, flinging my hand out to indicate what had happened downstairs. "I mean, I know this whole thing started with the stipulation that we'd break up after Thanksgiving, but you never said you were going to make a scene."

"Got the job done, didn't it?"

"But why, Ridge?" I asked, my voice quivering. "Why be such a dick about it, and then ... *go off with Caitlyn?*"

"Who cares? It's done," he answered, moving to flop on the bed.

"Why did it have to be done at all?" I asked, needing to know even if it hurt. "I thought we really had something. That we'd moved on from the pact."

Ridge looked at me through bleary eyes. "Yeah, me too. Guess we were both wrong."

I let out a strangled laugh.

"So, was it all just bullshit? You got me in bed, used me to piss off your mother, and that's it? It's over?"

"Look, I've been nothing but honest with you from the beginning. This was always gonna end ... At least I didn't pretend to be something I'm not."

"And, what, you're saying *I* did?"

I stood and crossed the floor to stare down at him, my hands on my hips.

"You sure as shit acted like you were into something more serious there at the end, but I heard what you told my sisters. It was all part of the game. *Fuck*, you couldn't even hold up your end of the bargain and keep your mouth shut, even though you knew I didn't want anyone to know about the pact ... especially my family."

"Is that why you're so mad? Because I told them?"

"I'm mad because you played me. Because I believed for a minute that you actually liked me for me ... not for my money, or my family, or what I could do for you ... but, in the end, you're just like everyone else."

"You heard my conversation with your sisters, and that's what you got out of it? That I was using you?"

"Mmmhmmm."

"And, that's why you're acting like a total jerk ... drinking too much and grabbing other girls? Humiliating me in front of everyone?"

"I always told you I was a dick," Ridge said reasonably, as if it made up for everything.

I scoffed. "How long have you been drinking?"

"Dunno, since Friday? What day is it?" he asked, and I felt my anger die off.

"You're right, you *are* a dick. You're also a fucking idiot."

"*Thanks*," Ridge said with as much sarcasm as he could muster.

I could tell he was about to pass out, so I leaned over him and said calmly, "If you'd stayed and listened to the whole conversation, you would have heard me say things had stopped being fake a while back, and I was falling in love with you."

The only response was a soft snore, so I left without a backwards glance.

THIRTY-SEVEN
RIDGE

Jesus!

It felt like someone bashed in my head with a sledgehammer.

I groaned audibly as I rolled over in bed. I was still fully dressed, on top of the covers, and there was drool on my duvet.

This is what rock bottom looks like.

My stomach revolted as I moved my feet to the floor and attempted to sit up. It ended up being more of a slide slash fall off the bed onto the floor kind of move. Not at all coordinated. And, the movement had bile rising in my throat as my skull pounded.

"Fuck," I muttered, no longer attempting to move. "I'll just sit here until it passes."

I'm not sure how long I sat on the floor, but it didn't pass. If anything, I felt worse. I wasn't sure what I drank, how much, or for how long, but even the thought of a drop of any alcohol crossing my lips was enough to have me heaving all over the floor.

I puked on my carpet, my pants, even my book bag, which was too close to the line of fire.

Wishing death would take me, I placed my hands on the bed and gingerly tried to rise to my feet without slipping in my own vomit.

I'd been wrong, *this* was what rock bottom looked like.

I managed to get myself into the shower, standing under the hot spray until I began to feel marginally human again, then went out to clean up my mess. I could have made a pledge do it, but not only was I not that much of an asshole, I was embarrassed enough to not want anyone to know what a mess I was.

Once I'd cleaned up as best I could, I opened my window to try and air out the stench of booze, sweat, and barf, and went downstairs in search of water and the most potent extra-strength headache medicine I could find.

Maybe some crackers.

I caught myself from falling halfway down the stairs and took the rest of the steps slowly, cautiously, my hand gripping the rail.

"*Holy shit!*" I exclaimed when I reached the bottom and looked around.

The house was trashed.

My hands flew to my head as I walked through, noting a hole in the wall, and debris everywhere.

"What the hell happened last night?" I asked the first pledge I came upon who was shoving empty beer cans into a large black trash bag.

"After you and that girl left things kinda went nuts. Crush came back, pissed about being kicked out of Delta. He punched the wall and started screaming about wanting to fight. He called out every brother, including you, but no one took him up on it, so he kept on breaking stuff."

"*Jesus*," I muttered, trying to remember the kid's name, but unable to think with the clanging in my head. "Wait, what girl did I leave with?"

I tried to think back, but came up blank.

"Uh, the really tall one ... she hangs around here a lot, always wearing something tight, to uh, show off her assets if you get what I mean."

"Bella? Caitlyn?" I asked, hoping like hell nothing happened. I mean, I'd woken up alone, but that didn't mean I started out that way.

"Yeah, *Caitlyn*, that's the one," he replied with a snap of his fingers. "Karrie didn't look too happy about it either, but I guess you don't care, since you broke up."

"*What?*" I asked, but flashes of the night started coming back to me.

Drinking ... lots of drinking.

Me yelling at Karrie and breaking up with her publicly.

Her standing there looking devastated, trying to get me to calm down and talk privately.

Pulling Caitlyn to me and leading her out of the party in hopes of making Karrie jealous.

Karrie waiting for me in my room.

And, the last thing I heard before passing out ... "*I was falling in love with you.*"

"*Fuck,*" I muttered, running my hand roughly over my face. "What did I do?"

"You basically told everyone she was just using you to get back at Drake, and to leave you alone and never come back to Delta."

I looked at him blandly.

"It was a rhetorical question."

"Oh, sorry," he said sheepishly and went back to cleaning up.

I turned and ran back upstairs, trying my best not to throw up again even though my stomach was jostled with every step.

I grabbed my wallet and keys and hurried back downstairs

to snag that water and medicine, before heading out to talk to Karrie.

I drove slowly, hoping like hell I didn't get pulled over, because with as much alcohol as I'd consumed over the weekend, I couldn't be sure I'd puked it all out. The last thing I needed was to get pulled over.

I made it to Karrie's in one piece and rushed to her apartment, not having the first clue what to say to make things right, only knowing I had to try.

I took a deep breath, hoping I didn't still have alcohol coming out of my pores, and raised my fist to knock on the door.

After a few seconds, I knocked again.

The door didn't open, but I thought I heard movement on the other side, so I placed my palm on the door, leaned in, and called, "Karrie?"

Nothing.

"Karrie, it's Ridge ... I just want to talk."

I stepped back when I heard the knob being turned, but instead of Karrie standing on the other side, Mina stood there, glaring back at me.

"Hey, Mina, is Karrie here?" I asked tentatively, hoping I wasn't about to get kicked in the balls, cause it kinda looked like she was leaning that way.

"Not for you," she replied, jutting her hip out and crossing her arms over her chest.

"Come on, Mina, I need to apologize and clear things up," I pleaded, not too proud to beg.

Mina nodded and agreed, "Yes, you do. But not right now ... not today. She needs some space to think."

"At least tell me if she's doing okay."

"She's fine, Ridge. What, do you think you broke her?" Mina chuckled dryly. "It'll take more than some asshole to keep my girl down. Now, I'm gonna close this door and you're going to go. You won't call or text Karrie, you'll give her the time she needs to figure out what she wants."

"I didn't mean it," I told her, needing to clear the air, even if it was with Karrie's best friend and not her. "I fucked up and acted like a jerk. I should have talked to her instead of flying off the handle. And, what I did last night ... I'm so fucking sorry."

"All of that is true, and Karrie being the sweet and compassionate person she is will probably hear you out and maybe even forgive you. But, not today. Got it?" she asked, and I would've been impressed by her loyalty and resolve if she wasn't what was standing in between me and Karrie.

"I got it," I replied, then sighed and turned to leave.

"Ridge," Mina called, and I turned back quickly, full of hope.

"Groveling, and presents ... *lots of presents*," she said, and shut the door.

THIRTY-EIGHT

KARRIE

"Karrie!"

I stopped my descent down the concrete steps and turned to see who was calling me.

I sighed as another Delta pledge came running over carrying a small pink bag with matching tissue paper sticking out.

"Oh, thank God, my next class is in five minutes and I worried I'd missed you," he said, shoving the bag at me.

I didn't want to make him late, so I took it, even though I had no intention of opening it. It could go on our kitchen counter along with the other three bags, two gift boxes, and four bouquets of flowers I'd received from Ridge over the last five days.

I continued across campus, head down, wondering if it was time for me to talk to Ridge. Mina had told me everything he'd said, even though it was unnecessary, since I'd been standing on the other side of the door, listening.

Still, I trusted her and wanted her perspective.

Although she was pissed at him, and wanted more information about why he acted the way he had, and thought he needed to do a lot of apologizing to make it up to me, she said she believed Ridge was sincere.

I just wasn't sure I was ready to face him yet.

"Karrie!"

I heard my name called again and stopped without looking around.

"*Seriously? If it's another pledge with a gift...*" I muttered under my breath. But, it wasn't a pledge, it was Drake.

Great.

"What do *you* want?" I asked, cinching my backpack tighter.

"Hey, how's it going?" Drake asked, smiling at me in the way I used to find charming.

"Fine," I replied curtly. "What's up?"

"Nothing, you on your way home?"

"Yeah."

"Cool, I'll walk with you," he said, and I looked at him in confusion.

"Why?"

Drake just grinned at me and fell into step next to me when I started walking. "So, I heard about the party at Delta last weekend. Pretty crazy..."

"Oh yeah?" I replied, not really wanting to talk to him about this ... or anything.

"Yup, and I have some good news."

"What's that?" I asked, picking up the pace in hopes of ending this walk sooner rather than later.

"I ended it with Sharna," he said, watching me expectantly.

"I assume Sharna's the girl you've been seeing," I replied, wondering why he was telling me this.

"Yup, and after I heard what Ridge said at the party, I realized what a mistake I'd made, so I ended it. Now we're free to get back together."

I stopped walking and my jaw dropped. "Say what now?"

"I know you were just with him to make me jealous, and I gotta tell you, I appreciate the effort. I mean, the fact that you loved me so much you were willing to hang around that asshole in order to make me crazy? It totally worked."

"You're kidding?" I said, because honestly, *what the hell?*

"No, I'm serious. Plus, you're shit hot ... I don't know what influence Ridge had on that, but I'm not mad about the sexy little outfits, especially if you're wearing them for me and not him."

I gaped at him, unable to respond.

"Hanging at Delta with Ridge and getting your little makeover really improved your clout. I think we could really be a power couple this time around," he added, and that was it, I wanted to punch him in his stupid face.

"*Clout?*" I asked, unable to take him seriously.

Drake nodded.

"So, whattaya say? Wanna hang out tonight?"

I blinked, then snapped my fingers in front of his face.

"*Wake up!* No, Drake, I do not want to hang out tonight, or any other night for that matter. I'm not pining for you and I don't want to get back together. I'm sorry if you believed something that Ridge said when he was drunk at a party, but the thought of being with you again just made me throw up in my mouth. You dumped me out of the blue, moved on immediately, and it turns out you were cheating on me during our entire relationship. I deserve better than you."

Drake's expression morphed from happy, to shocked, to pissed while I spoke. It would have been comical if I wasn't so frustrated.

"Like who, *Ridge?*" Drake scoffed, no longer *Mr. Nice Guy*. "Looks like he doesn't want you either. You ever think maybe you're the problem, Karrie?"

"You know what, Drake, I don't want to have this discussion with you anymore, and the great thing is ... I don't have to. Goodbye," I said, leaving him behind and jogging the rest of the way home.

I slammed into the apartment and threw the gift bag onto the counter.

"You good?" Mina asked, coming out to see what the commotion was about.

"Why are men so freakin' stupid?" I seethed.

"I think it has something to do with their cocks. It's really the only explanation."

THIRTY-NINE
RIDGE

"You okay?"

I looked up from my desk to see Wes standing in my doorway.

"Uh, yeah, pretty good. How 'bout you?" I asked, scooting my chair back and turning toward him.

He stepped into the room and put his hands in his pockets.

"I tried talking to Mom, but she's being stubborn. She insists she hasn't done anything wrong, and when I try to contradict her, she shuts down. I told her if she keeps it up, she'll end up alone."

"What'd she say to that?"

"She said, once Brody leaves, she'll be alone anyway, so what does it matter."

"If that's how she feels, then it's on her," I replied, just a tad bitter.

Wes sat on my bed and looked at me with eyes full of sorrow.

"I don't want that for her ... to be lonely for the rest of her life."

"You're a good son, and a good brother," I assured him. "I

won't hold it against you if you want to be a part of her life, Wes, it's totally up to you. Just don't get on my case about *not* being a part of it."

He nodded and asked, "Ya hear back from Karrie yet?"

"No, not yet," I admitted. "I'm trying to do what Mina asked and give her space while still letting her know that I'm here and eager to talk."

"You still sending gifts with pledges?"

I nodded.

"Yeah, so at least I know she's getting them, but for all I know she's throwing them away as soon as she's alone."

"Why don't you let me deliver the next one," he suggested.

"Really? Cause I have roses ready to be picked up in about fifteen minutes."

"Well, why don't we go pick them up and you can drive me to go give them to her."

"What if she sees me? I want to give her the space she needs ... I really don't want to screw up worse than I already have," I said, speaking honestly to my brother in a way I wouldn't to anyone else.

"Ridge, it's been five days. You've given her space and you've sent apology gifts. She hasn't come running back into your arms ready to forgive and forget. So, I think you need to change tactics. Let me talk to her. I'll explain what happened and see if she'll talk to you. If she says yes, you'll be there and can strike while the iron's hot."

"And if she says no?"

"Then she never has to know you were there waiting and you can keep doing what you're doing, or move on."

I don't want to move on ... I want Karrie back.

"Okay, let's do it," I said coming to my feet. "Just don't piss her off."

Wes agreed with a chuckle and we left to go and try and get my girl back.

Twenty minutes later, I was in the hallway, around the corner, leaning against the wall and more nervous than I'd ever been.

I heard Wes knock on the door and held my breath.

"Karrie, there's another one," I heard Mina yell, before saying, "Wait, you're one of Ridge's brothers, aren't you?"

Before he could reply, Karrie must have joined them, because I heard her say, "Wes, *hey*."

My heart gave a little pitter-patter at the sound of her voice and I thought, *Wow, Ridge, you're such a pussy*, but realized, I didn't care. If it would get her back, I'd write a love poem ... jump out of an airplane ... hell, I'd eat at the food court every night, if that's what she wanted.

"Hi, Karrie, this is from Ridge," Wes said, and I imagined he was handing her the roses.

"Thanks."

"Can I talk to you for a minute?" he asked. "Alone?"

There was a pause, where I was sure Mina was giving him a *hell no* look, but then Karrie said, "Sure. Can you give us a minute, Ermina?"

"Okay, but I'll be on the other side of this door," Mina replied.

"I'll protect her," Wes said wryly.

"It's okay," Karrie assured her best friend and self-appointed bodyguard.

I heard the door close and had to stop myself from rounding the corner and rushing to her.

"So..." Karrie prompted.

"How are you?" Wes asked.

"Oh, um, good, I guess," she replied, sounding surprised.

"Brody and I have been worried about you."

"You have?"

"Yeah, and I know our sisters would be, too, if they knew what was going on. We all really like you, Karrie, and think you're great for Ridge. You make him less of a pain in the ass," my *least favorite* brother said.

Karrie laughed lightly, and I yearned to see her face. "Don't be so hard on him."

"What about you?" Wes asked. "Will you stop being so hard on him?"

"Wes..."

"He fucked up, Karrie, Ridge knows it ... hell, everyone knows it. Let him apologize, talk shit out. I think you both need to get everything off your chest and out in the open. Because until you do, neither of you can move on ... whether it's together or apart."

"I'm scared," Karrie said, and it felt like she'd kicked me in the stomach. "The last time we were together, it wasn't good."

"He was a drunk angry asshole," Wes agreed ... *seriously?* "But, he's completely sober and only twenty-five percent asshole right now. How 'bout you give him a chance?"

"What, now? He's here?" she asked.

"Right around the corner," Wes said.

I forced myself to remain still, leaning against the wall as if I hadn't a care in the world, but my eyes watched greedily for her.

Karrie rounded the corner, and my breath caught.

She had on her Thirty Seconds to Mars T-shirt, cut-off sweats, and her hair was up in a messy bun.

She was the most gorgeous woman I'd ever seen.

FORTY

KARRIE

God, he looked beautiful.

I took him in head to toe, my heart telling me how much I'd missed him, but I kept my expression purposefully blank.

"Still holding up walls?" I asked, moving close, but not too close.

"Still dressing for comfort, not style?" he teased.

"Always."

Ridge pushed off the wall and stood before me.

"You look amazing," he said, sounding totally sincere.

"S*top*," I whispered, because, honestly, I couldn't handle sweet Ridge.

"I'm sorry, *so fucking sorry*, Karrie. I overreacted and lashed out with anger when I should have talked to you. Hell, if I hadn't acted like a titty baby and come out to breakfast rather than storming off to the bedroom, this whole shit show would have been avoided."

"This is true," I replied, trying so hard not to cave and launch myself into his arms.

"You are everything ... beautiful, smart, funny, and you don't let me get away with shit. I've been racking my brain trying to figure out the perfect thing to give you to show you how sorry I am, but knowing you the way I do, I know there's no such physical thing. You don't care about money or gifts, you care about actions and words."

My eyes filled as Ridge spoke. The way he got me was a beautiful thing, and not something I'd encountered with anyone other than my family and Mina.

He reached out and brushed away an errant tear and my eyes drifted shut at the soft touch.

"The things I said to you at Delta were unforgiveable, but I'm going to ask you to forgive me anyway, because this last week has been the worst of my life. I don't know how I got through the first twenty-one years without you, but now that I know what being with you is like, I can't be without you."

"I've missed you, too," I admitted, because, *yeah*, I was totally caving.

"My brothers are the only people who have ever loved me in my life, so I didn't know what it looked like coming from you. I didn't trust my heart, but rather listened to the skeptical part of my brain, and did a disservice to us both."

Yup, I was full-on crying now.

"If you'll give me another shot, I promise to never make assumptions, never eavesdrop on conversations and believe the worst. I'll talk to you, about everything ... about so much you'll beg me to stop being so open, but I won't listen. I'll allow myself to experience your love, and I'll show you mine in return. Because, although I may be a novice, I'm a quick learner, and I swear I'll love you better than anyone has before me, or ever will after."

"Ridge," I managed, my voice shaking.

"Can you ever forgive me?" he asked, his face full of fear.

I'd never seen Ridge afraid of anything, and it was his

vulnerability that did it.

"Yes, I can," I began, taking a deep breath to steady myself before adding, "But, you really hurt me, Ridge. And, although I know it's unrealistic to think we won't hurt each other, I need to know you're not going to go rogue like that again. Talk to me ... that's all I ask."

"I promise."

"Okay ... I forgive you, and, Ridge, I love you, too, even when you're an idiot."

Ridge pulled me into his arms and hugged me tightly.

"What about when I'm a dick?" he asked against my hair.

"Even then."

"What about..."

"Don't push it," I said with a laugh, reaching up to pull him down for a kiss.

It started slow, sweet, a little desperate, and quickly became heated. We expressed how much we missed each other through our lips, the touch of his hand on my lower back, the squeeze from mine on his perfectly formed ass.

"Well, that escalated quickly," Wes said from behind us, causing us to break the kiss.

I dropped my head against Ridge's chest and laughed.

"Hey, does this mean we can open the presents now?" Mina asked.

I shifted to see both of them standing at the end of the hall, watching us with smiling faces.

"You never opened them?" Ridge asked.

I looked up at him and shook my head. "I wasn't ready," I admitted.

"Are you ready now?" Mina asked hopefully.

"Sure, let's do it," I said, taking Ridge's hand in mine as we followed Wes and Mina into our apartment.

As soon as we were all in the kitchen, Mina picked up a bag

and thrust it at me.

"Here, this one's the heaviest," she said.

I reached in, wishing I'd opened these before, because I was a bit embarrassed opening them in front of Ridge and Wes. I'd never been the kid who liked to be the center of attention and open all of her birthday presents at her party.

"*Oh my God, you didn't,*" I exclaimed, embarrassment forgotten as I pulled out a framed signed Thirty Seconds to Mars C.D. and album cover. "Where did you find this?"

"I'll never tell," Ridge said with a grin, obviously pleased at my excitement.

"Now I need to know what's in the rest," Mina said, shoving presents at me.

Other than the flowers, Ridge hadn't given me any of the traditional presents I'd expected. There was no jewelry or candy, instead I had a new softball glove, a cookbook with a Philly cheesesteak on the cover, an old *Wayne's World* DVD, some scrunchies, and...

"What's this?" I asked, holding up a piece of paper.

"It's the logon and password to your new Spotify account. I made you a playlist."

"Like ... a mixtape?" I asked, reaching for my phone so I could sign out and log in to the new account.

Ridge was quiet as I scrolled down the playlist.

When I was done, I leaned into him and placed my hand over his heart.

"For someone who claims not to know about love, you sure know how to make a girl swoon. It's perfect."

"I figured I can keep adding to it, whenever I hear something that reminds me of you. You should have over a million songs, before it's all said and done."

"I'm gonna love you so hard," I promised.

"I'll hold you to it."

EPILOGUE

"We're so glad you all came to help us celebrate tonight. These guys have been working hard and tirelessly to fulfill all of the duties as pledge and become full-fledged members. And, now, I'm happy to introduce you to the newest Deltas..."

We were once again at Delta house, this time to be there for Wes as he joined Ridge as a Delta brother.

"Do you think Brody will want to pledge next year?" I asked Ridge, who was in his usual spot, perched on a wall in the living room.

He looked so handsome with his blue button down making his eyes pop, and sporting a new closely shaven beard. If anything, the beard made him look manlier, and sexier, and it felt wonderful when he was between my thighs.

But, I digress...

"I think so," Ridge said, his hand moving down to cup my ass. "Honestly, I'll just be happy he's here, no matter whether he decides to rush or not. It'll be great to see him more."

"Is Wes still planning to move into the house?"

"Yeah, I was thinking of telling him he could have my room," he replied.

"Really? Like you'll share?" I asked, having a hard time picturing Ridge with a roommate, even if it was his brother.

It would definitely put a wrench in our alone time if he did ... oh well, we'd just spend more nights at my place.

"No," Ridge laughed. "I was thinking of moving out altogether, maybe getting a place with my girlfriend."

My mouth dropped open as I looked up at him. "What? You want to move in together?"

My stomach was a flutter with nerves and something else ... excitement maybe?

"If you'll say yes, absolutely. I was thinking we could get a little house off campus, or maybe a condo. I don't know yet, but if you're game I'll start looking tomorrow."

"A house or a condo?"

I knew I was repeating everything he said, but I couldn't help it, I was completely surprised.

Ridge chuckled and brought his hand up to cup my cheek.

"A house, condo, apartment, treehouse ... it really doesn't matter to me, as long as you're there with me."

Oh, boy.

"Okay, but it has to be something affordable, so that I can pitch in. You're not going to be my sugar daddy," I insisted.

"We're going to find somewhere safe, in a good neighborhood, no matter the cost," Ridge argued, and I was about to put my foot down when he said, "That part is non-negotiable. I won't move you somewhere unless I'm sure you'll be safe. But, we can work it out where you pay utilities, or groceries. I know you want to contribute, but, babe, you do. It's not just about money."

"I know that," I said, and I did ... still, "I don't want it to seem like I'm taking advantage."

"To whom?" Ridge asked. "Because, you and I know you're not, and no one else fucking matters, so..."

I smiled, because, he was right. No one who mattered would even worry about who was paying our rent. Not my family, or his brothers. But, I couldn't help but worry about his parents and what they thought, even if he didn't.

But, since they hadn't even contacted him in the time I'd known him, I needed to trust his judgement and not take their opinions into consideration.

It made me sad, but it also made me love him that much more.

Because ... he deserved it. We both did.

RIDGE'S PLAYLIST

Happier by Ed Sheeran
Be Alright by Dean Lewis
Come As You Are by Nirvana
The Kill by Thirty Seconds to Mars
Bohemian Rhapsody by Queen
All of Me by John Legend
Eastside by Halsey, Khalid, and Benny Blanco
Sucker by Jonas
When the Party's Over by Billie Eilish

Want to learn more about Ridge's sisters? Check out the Three Sisters Catering Trilogy. Starting with A Pinch of Salt.

Curious about how Karrie's parents got together? Read their story in Indelible.

FRAT HOUSE CONFESSIONS: WES

Prologue

"So, how does this work?" I asked Papi, Delta's Treasurer and resident advice giver.

"Well, some of the guys like to play up the priest angle, while others come in and lay on my couch like I'm a damn therapist. Personally, I'd rather you just lay out your issue and we'll move forward from there," Papi replied, glancing at me briefly before focusing on the arm curls he was currently doing. "Although, with you, little Ridge, I'm pretty sure I already know the issue."

I masked my expression, not wanting to show my displeasure at the nickname *little Ridge* for fear he'd kick me out and not help me.

Papi, real name Hector, had originally planned to become a priest, hence his in-room confessional. Rumor had it that once he got old enough to realize everything he'd be missing out on by joining the priesthood, he'd devastated his parents by becoming the polar opposite.

I could attest that the ladies did go crazy over the tall, dark, and super yoked senior.

"Yeah, you do... everyone does, that's the problem. I've become the butt of everyone's jokes at Delta. I want to make it right and prove last year was a fluke, that I belong here, just like everyone else."

It was hard, being the younger brother of the Delta President, and the guy who'd been duped by an undercover school journalist during rush.

I'd thought Trixie was my friend. We'd met in class and she'd agreed to help me out with this makeover challenge, if I agreed to teach her how to pick up chicks. That should have been my first clue. Trixie was funny, smart, and edgy in a way I'd never be, plus, she probably had more game in her little finger than I had in my whole body.

Still, it was nice to feel needed, so I'd stupidly believed what she said and we'd struck up a deal. Little did I know, it had all been bullshit. The entire time I thought we were friends, she'd been writing an expose on the competition, Delta, and Crush, the misogynistic asshole who used to be our VP.

After she and I had one the competition, she'd come clean with me, and I'd immediately told Ridge. After talking to our then President, we'd gone to talk to her and asked her to keep the Delta name out of it.

She'd agreed, but the story had still run the next week and Crush had been kicked out of Delta.

I hadn't spoken with her since.

Papi placed the weights on the floor and turned his attention to me. He watched me quietly, and if I hadn't seen him do the same countless times when he was thinking, I'd have been freaked out by the directness of his stare.

Papi intimidated the shit out of me. But then, most of the high ranked Delta's did.

After a few moments, he snapped his fingers and said, "The way I see it, you have two options."

I leaned forward, resting my forearms on my knees and said eagerly, "I'm listening."

"Either, you can bring her around, show her how wrong she was about the guys and the frat, and let the guys get to know her, too. Let them see why you trusted her, and have her come clean, tell them you had no idea what she was about."

I really didn't think she would go for that, so I asked, "What's the other option?"

"A little quid pro quo... make her fall in love with you, hard, then dump her."

I blinked, cause that sounded pretty harsh. I didn't say that though, lord knew the Papi already thought I was a pussy... instead I shook my head and said, "I'm pretty sure she's still dating someone, a girl. I mean, she is bi, but I don't think she's the kind of guy she'd go for."

"So, become that guy, Wes. She'll never see you coming."

I pursed my lips, not really sure if either option would work.

Papi stood up, grabbed a towel and wiped it over his head and face.

"If you want the guys to stop harassing you, and be seen as someone other than little Ridge, the guy who let a reporter into our midst, these are your best options. As with any penance, it's up to you to follow through and do the work. Now, I'm gonna hit the showers."

I got to my feet.

"Thanks, Papi, I'll take what you said into consideration."

"Wes," he called when I was almost to the door.

I turned back and he said, "Who you are, how you're perceived, and how your college experience plays out is completely up to you. You're in charge of your own destiny. You can do this, bro, I have faith in you."

"Thanks, Papi," I replied and walked out, shutting the door behind me.

I didn't think I could get her to come hang out at Delta, not after reading that article. It was pretty obvious she hated frats and thought any guy in one was a complete asshole. Plus, I didn't see the guys welcoming her with open arms. Still, that seemed more plausible than getting her to fall in love with me.

Shit, I thought, feeling bummed that Papi's advice hadn't been some magical cure that fixed everything.

I guess I had some more thinking to do, and Papi *was* right about one thing, the only person who could fix this mess I'd landed in, was me.

COMING SOON!

ABOUT THE AUTHOR

Bethany Lopez is a USA Today Bestselling author of more than thirty books and has been published since 2011. She's a lover of all things romance, which she incorporates into the books she writes, no matter the genre.

When she isn't reading or writing, she loves spending time with family and traveling whenever possible.

Bethany can usually be found with a cup of coffee or glass of wine at hand, and will never turn down a cupcake!

To learn more about upcoming events and releases, sign up for my newsletter.

www.bethanylopezauthor.com
bethanylopezauthor@gmail.com

Follow her at https://www.bookbub.com/authors/bethany-lopez *to get an alert whenever she has a new release, preorder, or discount!*

ALSO BY BETHANY LOPEZ

Contemporary Romance:

A Time for Love Series

Prequel - 1 Night

8 Weeks

21 Days

42 Hours

15 Minutes

10 Years

3 Seconds

7 Months

For Eternity - Novella

Night & Day - Novella

The Lewis Cousins Series

Too Tempting

Too Complicated

Too Distracting

Too Enchanting

Too Dangerous

Three Sisters Catering Trilogy

A Pinch of Salt

A Touch of Cinnamon

A Splash of Vanilla

Frat House Confessions

Frat House Confessions: Ridge

Romantic Comedy/Suspense:

Cupcakes Series

Always Room for Cupcakes

Cupcake Overload

Lei'd with Cupcakes

Cupcake Explosion

Lei'd in Paradise - Novella

Women's Fiction:

More than Exist

Unwoven Ties - Newsletter Exclusive

Short Stories:

Contemporary:

Christmas Come Early

Harem Night

Reunion Fling

An Inconvenient Dare

Fantasy:

Leap of Faith

Beau and the Beastess

Cookbook:

Love & Recipes

Love & Cupcakes

Children's:

Katie and the North Star

Young Adult:

Stories about Melissa – series

Ta Ta for Now!

xoxoxo

Ciao

TTYL

With Love

Adios

Young Adult Fantasy:

Nissa: a contemporary fairy tale

New Adult:

Friends & Lovers Trilogy

Make it Last

I Choose You

Trust in Me

Indelible

Made in the USA
Columbia, SC
19 September 2019